A MONTANA COWBOY

—

REBECCA WINTERS

HARLEQUIN® AMERICAN ROMANCE®

Recycling programs
for this product may
not exist in your area.

ISBN-13: 978-0-373-75563-9

A Montana Cowboy

Copyright © 2015 by Rebecca Winters

All rights reserved. Except for use in any review, the reproduction or
utilization of this work in whole or in part in any form by any electronic,
mechanical or other means, now known or hereinafter invented, including
xerography, photocopying and recording, or in any information storage
or retrieval system, is forbidden without the written permission of the
publisher, Harlequin Enterprises Limited, 225 Duncan Mill Road,
Don Mills, Ontario M3B 3K9, Canada.

This is a work of fiction. Names, characters, places and incidents are
either the product of the author's imagination or are used fictitiously,
and any resemblance to actual persons, living or dead, business
establishments, events or locales is entirely coincidental.

This edition published by arrangement with Harlequin Books S.A.

For questions and comments about the quality of this book,
please contact us at CustomerService@Harlequin.com.

® and TM are trademarks of Harlequin Enterprises Limited or its
corporate affiliates. Trademarks indicated with ® are registered in the
United States Patent and Trademark Office, the Canadian Intellectual
Property Office and in other countries.

Printed in U.S.A.

"You're so good to me."

Their mouths were achingly close. He brushed his lips against hers out of need. "It's because you're so easy to please I want to do everything for you."

"Trace..." This time she took the initiative and pressed her lips against his. That was all it took to deprive him of his last shred of self-control. Maybe he was dreaming, but her mouth seemed to welcome his, urging him to kiss her and hold nothing back.

He pulled her against him, loving the shape of her, the fragrance of her hair, the softness of her skin. She'd aroused his passion on so many levels, he didn't know how he was going to stop, but he had to. He could feel her baby. Much as he wanted to make love to her, he couldn't. This wasn't the time, or the place. Cassie needed to be able to trust him.

Let go of her now, Rafferty.

Dear Reader,

Second chances...

Everyone deserves a second chance because none of us is perfect. No plan for life is perfect, either, right?

Take, for example, the couple in my final book of the Hitting Rocks Cowboys series, *A Montana Cowboy*. Trace has been injured on a mission and can no longer pursue his dream of being a military pilot. Cassie, a woman without a home, has lost her husband and is now pregnant and facing the unknown. Both of these people have experienced great pain. At this precarious crossroads in both their lives, chance has brought them together. I hope you'll enjoy watching them come to know each other, while they simultaneously battle a menace that ultimately unites them...and brings them to a whole new level of happiness they hadn't thought possible.

Enjoy!

Rebecca Winters

Rebecca Winters, whose family of four children has now swelled to include five beautiful grandchildren, lives in Salt Lake City, Utah, in the land of the Rocky Mountains. With canyons and high alpine meadows full of wildflowers, she never runs out of places to explore. They, plus her favorite vacation spots in Europe, often end up as backgrounds for her romance novels, because writing is her passion, along with her family and church.

Rebecca loves to hear from readers. If you wish to email her, please visit her website, cleanromances.com.

Books by Rebecca Winters

HARLEQUIN AMERICAN ROMANCE

Hitting Rocks Cowboys

In a Cowboy's Arms
A Cowboy's Heart
The New Cowboy

Daddy Dude Ranch

The Wyoming Cowboy
Home to Wyoming
Her Wyoming Hero

Undercover Heroes

The SEAL's Promise
The Marshal's Prize
The Texas Ranger's Reward

This and other titles by Rebecca Winters are also available in ebook format from Harlequin.com.

To my editor Kathleen, who allows me
to write the books of my heart. What joy!

Chapter One

Captain Trace Rafferty of the Thirty-First Fighter Wing out of Aviano Air Base was coming home for good, much sooner than he'd expected.

Since leaving Italy, where his squadron had flown F-16s critical to operations in NATO's southern region, he'd been in Colorado Springs, Colorado, for the past few days talking with the higher-ups. Having been forced to retire as a jet pilot from the Air Force at twenty-eight due to an eye injury, he'd decided to accept a flight instructor position at the Air Force Academy.

Trace had been asked to stay on with the Thirty-First as a flight navigator, but after being a pilot, he couldn't do it. The Academy was giving him time to get his affairs in order before he went to work for them. He would use this time to tell his father about his future plans... plans his father wasn't going to be happy about.

Sam Rafferty, known as Doc, was a cowboy and rancher besides being the head veterinarian in White Lodge, Montana. A year ago he'd married Ellen Neerings, a pretty brunette widow from the same town, and they lived in a condo. His arthritic hips had made it impossible for him to live and take care of things on the ranch any longer.

Ellen's husband had died several years earlier. With the sale of their small family home, she'd been able to pay off mounting debts because of her husband's long illness, but she'd been left with little to live on.

Both she and Trace's father had sacrificed too much for their families. His dad should have the money from the sale of the ranch to buy him and Ellen a new house of their own in White Lodge with every convenience. She had two married children and needed more space for them and her grandchildren when they came to visit from other parts of the state.

Since Trace wasn't going to live in Montana, selling the ranch was the only sensible solution to make his father's life more comfortable, but he knew it was a subject that would bring his dad pain. The ranch, located in the south central part of the state bordering Wyoming, had been in the Rafferty family for close to a hundred years. Trace hated the fact that his father had done so much for him all his life, virtually supporting him and his mother, even after she'd remarried. It was Trace's turn to give back.

His parents had divorced when he was eight years old. His mother had settled in Billings, only forty minutes away, taking him with her. She didn't like the ranch's isolation and preferred the amenities of living in town.

His dad had moved heaven and earth to be with his son as much as possible during those years. After living with such a kind, laid-back father, it had been hard for Trace to adjust to being around the rigid-type man his mother married soon after the divorce. When Trace turned eighteen, he joined the air force. His mom now lived in Oregon with her husband.

Trace hadn't come back to the United States very often and traveled home to visit his parents on his infrequent leaves. Over the past year the ranch had stood empty. While no one lived there, his dad had hired a former ranch hand named Logan Dorney from the neighboring Bannock ranch to be the foreman on the place until Trace claimed it for his inheritance. But Trace learned the other man had been accidentally killed by a stray bullet from a hunter in February.

Except for Logan's widow, Cassie Dorney, formerly Cassie Bannock, who came in to do the housekeeping once in a while, the ranch no longer had a foreman. Trace would take over that job until the place was sold. Again, all this had to be discussed with his father who knew nothing yet about Trace's plans.

When the fasten-seat-belt sign flashed on, he'd been deep in thought. It surprised him that the flight from Denver to Montana had been so short. He looked out the window. As the plane made its descent to the Billings airport, he decided summer was the best time to see the patches of wheat and corn fields. Below him lay a different mosaic from the farms dotting the Italian countryside he'd so recently left.

Soon the Yellowstone River came into view under a June sun. The airport itself sat on top of Rimrock, a unique five-hundred-foot-tall sandstone feature rising from the valley floor. It all looked familiar, but Trace felt little sense of homecoming.

After the jet landed and he'd picked up his bags, he grabbed a taxi and asked the driver to take him to the Marlow Ford dealership where he'd arranged to have his new Ford Explorer waiting for him. He inspected the vehicle and liked its Kodiak-brown color.

Trace took off for White Lodge, anxious to spend a little quality time with his father. It had been six months since they'd last seen each other. But when he dropped by the vet clinic, the new vet, Clive Masters, who'd replaced Liz Henson since her marriage to Connor Bannock, said Trace's dad was out on an emergency.

The world he'd once known kept going through changes. You couldn't go back and find everything the same. He understood that, but the thought added to his depression.

"Doc Rafferty has been expecting you. He said if you came while he was gone, he wants you to drive out to the ranch and get settled. When he's through, he'll meet you there."

"Good enough. Nice to meet you, Clive."

"I guess you know your dad thinks the world of you."

"He's my hero," Trace replied, which was only the truth. "See you again soon."

Trace got back in the Explorer and headed for the ranch bordering the Bannock's huge spread outside White Lodge.

For the past few years his dad had opened up the Rafferty property to seasonal hunters with permits. Whenever Trace thought about the ranch, it filled him with remembered pain over his parents' divorce and the move to Billings, wrenching him away from his dad. At least when he started work in Colorado, he'd be able to see his dad a lot more often as Sam and Ellen could drive over to visit him.

The old ranch house with the deep porch was set back from the road in the forested area. Two streams running brook trout and cutthroats ran through it. A perimeter dirt road to the side of the property led past crop land that opened up into pasture where cattle could graze. At one time his father had done it all, and had grown alfalfa and barley besides, but that portion lay fallow now.

To reach the house, you took the right fork in the road. There was only one other road before you reached it. This one led to an abandoned logging site and trailed into national forest land. At least here nothing looked changed about the area until he came in sight of the house.

He put on his brakes. At first he thought he must have come to the wrong place. The old log cabin had been freshly stained. Its big picture window and the attic window were now framed by exterior wooden shutters exquisitely hand painted with wildflowers of every color.

The addition of white wicker porch furniture with pale yellow padding and several large baskets of multicolored flowers hanging beneath the eaves added bright spots of color. He found that the changes transformed the place, making it inviting in a way it had never been before.

His father must have hired a decorator from town

to come out and get all this ready in order to welcome Trace home. The knowledge filled him with guilt over what he planned to do. Those years of working on the ranch with him on visitation were over. Sam Rafferty's cowboy son wasn't a cowboy anymore.

Curious to know who was responsible for the actual transformation of the house, he parked around the side next to an unfamiliar green pickup truck. He jumped down from the cab. The barn in back had been freshly stained, too. Everything looked in fabulous shape!

He walked around behind it where his dad had built a kennel for their dog, which stood empty now. Remembered pain propelled Trace back to the front door of the house. He knocked. Even though he had a key to get in, he'd seen the truck and didn't want to walk in unannounced on whoever was here. While he waited, he admired the professional quality of the artwork on the panels.

They reminded him of the shutters you saw on hundreds of alpine-style homes in the Alps. Trace never dreamed his father would go to this extent to make him excited about being home for good.

When no one answered the door, he left the porch and walked around the other side of the house where he was met with another surprise. The ground cover that had always grown next to the house had been cleared to accommodate a well-tended garden full of strawberry plants and raspberry bushes planted in rows. The strawberries looked ripe for the picking and smelled delicious on this hot Tuesday afternoon.

Trace caught a glimpse of someone working between

the rows. Curious to know who was there, he walked down one of them. As he got closer he saw it was a woman with wavy blond hair to the shoulders, gilded by the sun.

"Hello?" he called to her.

She lifted her head and got to her feet, holding a basket under her arm partially filled with strawberries. The raspberries hadn't ripened completely yet. The last time Trace had seen Cassie Bannock she was in her early teens. It strained the imagination that anyone in the well-heeled Bannock clan would be working as a housekeeper.

When Trace could sit down with his father, he'd find out the whole story behind it, but first things first. She was of medium height, her well-endowed body filled out an aqua-colored cotton top she wore over a pair of jeans. On her feet she wore cowboy boots. He found himself staring at her. She was blooming with health. He'd heard the term before, but she personified it.

"Captain Rafferty!"

"Call me Trace."

She laughed gently. "I couldn't resist. I've never met a jet pilot before." Her light green eyes smiled as she moved toward him. "You probably don't remember me."

Her coloring was different from that of her brunette cousin, Avery Lawson, another Bannock who was now married. But they both had the natural beauty of the Bannock genes in the classic shape of their faces and more voluptuous figures. Both were the same age, twenty-six or twenty-seven by now as he recalled.

"Of course I do. The last time I saw you I think you

were about twelve to my thirteen. You'd come with your grandfather Tyson to the vet clinic because your pet colt was sick and there was no consoling you. I was helping my dad and went to work with him that day."

"I'm surprised you remembered that. Sam got him all better. He's the best!"

"I agree," he murmured. "I'm very sorry to hear of your husband's unexpected passing."

A shadow crossed over her lovely face for a moment. She studied his features. "Thank you. I'm sorry to learn of your eye injury. Are you in pain?"

"No."

"Thank goodness for that at least." She had a sweetness about her. "Life throws all of us a curve once in a while, one we weren't expecting."

"You're right about that." Their losses were different. Though his career was over, he could still see with a corrective lens. Her loss had to be excruciating. According to Trace's father, they'd been a happily married couple while they'd worked for him.

"Your dad was afraid you might have to stay in the hospital longer for more tests."

"I received excellent care and was discharged the moment the doctor felt I could travel."

"That's wonderful and he's so excited! He said you'd be here today, but I expected the two of you to arrive this evening with you still wearing a uniform."

"The military doesn't usually travel in uniform these days. It's safer." She nodded. "My father said he'd meet up with me here later."

"Then welcome home, soldier. Go on in. Your old

bedroom is waiting for you. There's food and drinks in the fridge in case you're hungry or thirsty. Sam said you're a big tuna fish sandwich man, so there's plenty on hand. In case you need anything else, I'll be in as soon as I've filled this basket."

Berry-picking looked fun and Trace considered helping her, then thought the better of it. His gaze fell to her left hand. She still wore her wedding ring.

"Thank you, Cassie. See you shortly."

He retraced his steps to get his bags out of the Explorer. When he walked inside, the delicious aroma of strawberries filled the house. He moved through the foyer and dining room to the kitchen. She'd been making jam. Trace didn't realize her housekeeping duties extended to actually putting up fruit in a house where no one lived.

There were several dozen jars on the counter already filled and labeled. The sweet smell reminded him of times he'd played with the Bannock brothers as a boy before his parents' divorce. The last summer he'd lived here while he was still happy, he remembered going over to their grandmother's house where she was putting up jam and jelly. She'd let them pile butter and fresh jam on homemade bread and feast their heads off.

The wonderful memory pierced him. Soon after that time he'd learned his parents were divorcing and he'd have to move away from friends like Connor and Jarod Bannock, who lived next door. That turned out to be the darkest day of his young life. He'd been searching for happiness ever since. Being a pilot had given him thrills and purpose, but life had a habit of getting in the way.

He left the kitchen and walked across the hall to his bedroom to get rid of his bags. The same framed photographs of family that had always hung there lined the walls. It hurt to look at them. On the way he passed the other two bedrooms. One was his father's. The other was a spare bedroom, but when he looked inside, he received a shock rather than a surprise.

Cassie *lived* here?

Trace had assumed she'd moved back to the Bannock ranch with her family after her husband's death. Their wealth meant she wouldn't have financial worries. Maybe his kindhearted father had allowed her to stay on for a time while she worked through her grief. That was something he would do. If that were the case, then Trace's plan to sell the ranch would come as a blow to her while she was attempting to get through the worst of her pain. Hell...

That was another subject to talk over with his father when he arrived. But right now Trace was starving. The thought of a tuna fish sandwich on American soft white bread sounded so good, he headed straight back to the kitchen.

CASSIE HAD WATCHED his tall, well-honed physique, dressed in khakis and a crewneck shirt, disappear around the corner of the house. Trace Rafferty had been born an exceptionally handsome man. Judging from the photographs Sam had shown her after his son had gone into the military, time had only added to his male attributes. He'd inherited his mother's black hair and smile. But his rugged features and those searing hot blue eyes fringed by black lashes had come straight from his father.

Sam was so proud of his son, who'd served in many places around the globe. In or out of uniform, Trace Rafferty, still unmarried, possessed killer looks that would always cause him to stand out.

Cassie had been putting up jam for the past week, a little at a time. It always made the house smell good, so she'd decided to put up some more today to make his homecoming a little more welcoming. After that she'd started dinner with a pot roast in the oven and home-made rolls that were still rising.

According to Doc Rafferty, Trace hadn't been out to the ranch since his father had gotten married last year. On his last leave, he'd stayed in town with him and his new wife at their condo in White Lodge.

Perhaps it had been too painful to return to the home that was now empty of all family. But Sam had left it to his son and hoped he would make his life here now that he was out of the air force. She knew Sam's heart. He'd missed his son horribly over the years. To have him back home to stay would thrill him.

After finding as many ripe strawberries as she could, she made her way to the back door through the laundry room to the kitchen. Trace could have them fresh for breakfast if he wanted.

The minute she stepped in the kitchen, the first thing she noticed was the smell of tuna fish mingled with the jam aroma. Looking around she discovered Trace over in the corner at the breakfast table eating sandwiches.

He'd already drunk half a quart of milk without the aid of a glass.

He flashed her a smile that gave her an odd, fluttery sensation. "You've caught me."

Troubled that his smile had any effect on her at all, she put the basket of berries on the counter. "It's your house. You're entitled to do whatever you want."

"I didn't know you were still living here."

Uh oh. "After Logan died, I didn't plan to stay on, but your father insisted because he wanted the house kept up while no one was living here. Now that you're home, I plan to leave tonight after I've served you two dinner."

Though she hadn't told Sam yet, she'd already made arrangements with her cousin Avery to stay with her and her husband, Zane, until she found another place to live and work.

He shook his dark head. "Since I just arrived and don't know my own plans yet, I wouldn't dream of asking you to move out."

"But—"

"No buts. You were hired to take care of the house. From what I've already seen, you've done a fantastic job."

"Thank you." She checked on the roast, then started to leave the kitchen, almost faint with relief that she didn't have to give up this job quite yet.

"Where are you going?"

"I'm taking the horses for their daily exercise."

Trace emptied the milk bottle. His eyes played over her. "How do you manage that?"

She couldn't help but smile at the remark. "I ride

Buttercup and string Masala along. He goes where she goes."

"So he has a crush on her?"

A chuckle escaped her. "No. But he has no choice if he wants to leave the paddock. He's a wild mustang my cousin Connor tamed and gave to us. Besides Connor and your father, my husband was the only other man to ride him."

He continued to study her. "All you Bannocks are expert horse people. I'm surprised you haven't won that horse over yet."

She averted her eyes. "Masala preferred Logan."

Since when did that matter when according to Trace's father she was an expert horsewoman? He got up from the table. "If you don't mind, I'd like to come with you and take a look around the property. Maybe Masala will let me ride him. If not, I'll hold the rope and lead him around as we walk. After my flight, I need to stretch my legs."

Cassie preferred to be alone, but she didn't see how she could turn down Trace's offer. "Won't your father be here before long?"

"I don't know. Clive Masters said he'd gone out on an emergency. I'll text him to let him know we'll be back soon. If he's hungry, I made enough tuna fish for him to have some, too."

"He'll like that," she said. It seemed Trace had made up his mind. He had the confidence and authority of a man who was comfortable in any setting. "I'll meet you at the barn in a few minutes."

After she left the kitchen, Trace cleaned up the mess

he'd made and went back to his bedroom to put on jeans
and a T-shirt. His room was exactly as he'd left it. The
framed pictures of him, a couple with his dog, some
with his parents and some with Jarod and Connor out
horseback riding, still hung on the wall.

He found his old pair of cowboy boots and put them
on. With the exception of the last time he'd been home,
he and his father had always gone riding after chores
were done.

His ancient black cowboy hat sat on the closet shelf.
He dusted it off and shoved it on his head. Once he'd
sent his father a text, he headed for the barn. Cassie was
already out in the paddock astride her horse.

Buttercup was well named. Between Cassie's hair
and the palomino's golden color that included a white
mane and tail, they made quite a sight in the sun. He
rubbed her horse's forelock. "You're a real beauty, aren't
you Buttercup," he said, struggling not to look at Cassie.
Her coloring was the complete opposite from the Ital-
ians he'd spent time with over the past eighteen months.

Nicoletta Tornielli, the olive-skinned woman he'd
been planning to marry, had long black hair and large
black-brown eyes. After being around her family,
Cassie's fairness with that peaches-and-cream com-
plexion was in complete contrast.

While he was deep in thought over the change in
his circumstances, her horse pushed against his chest,
causing both of them to laugh. She smiled down at him.
"Buttercup likes you. When one of the older ranchers
in the area told Connor he needed to sell a couple of
his horses, Connor took me with him and I ended up

buying Buttercup. She's been a wonderful horse so far. Friendly."

"Your cousin has a great eye for horseflesh. One horse down, one to go." Still feeling her smile, he walked into the barn. The smell of the barn brought back memories of getting up early in the morning. He'd repair the fencing bordering the Bannock property with his father, or make certain the planted forage wasn't flooded by the numerous springs. Then he'd ride to the pasture. His job was to look for heifers in trouble while his dad checked on the rest of the herd.

In one of the stalls he found a blue roan with transverse stripes across the withers, marking him a wild mustang. "Hey, big fella." Trace started talking to the horse, touching him, using all the tricks his horse-loving father had taught him years ago. The gentleness paid off. Soon the horse was nickering. Trace went into the tack room for a bridle and brought it out.

At first Masala shied away from it, but Trace continued to talk to him in soothing tones until the horse allowed the bridle to be put on. "It's now or never," he muttered before mounting him. Trace had always preferred riding bareback on his favorite mount, Prince. That seemed a century ago. If this horse didn't like the weight, it was too late now.

Masala tossed his head several times and backed up, but when he realized he wasn't in charge, Trace made a clicking sound and rode him out of the barn.

Cassie's eyes flashed like green gemstones. "I don't believe it! I didn't think he'd let anyone else ride him."

"My father taught me a few techniques." They left

the paddock and headed for the deep forest that made the Rafferty property so desirable to Trace.

"You learned them well. He must sense the take-charge pilot in you."

"You think?" he teased.

"I know."

They rode side by side, following a faint trail that wound through the trees. With the temperature at eighty-one degrees, he welcomed the cool of the forest. When the fall hunting season was on, the abundance of wildlife made the property a big game hunter's paradise—elk, moose, mule deer, bison, white-tailed deer, bear and bighorn sheep roamed this part of the state. This ranch had it all. Someone would pay a lot of money for the property. Trace was determined that money would go right into his father's bank account.

He glanced over at Cassie. "Tell me something. Who did the work and staining on the exterior of the cabin? When I first drove in, I thought I'd come to the wrong house. It's so changed I hardly recognized it."

"That was Logan's doing."

"The artwork on the shutters, too?"

"No. That was my contribution."

Trace marveled at her skill. He took a deep breath of the pine-scented air. "And the garden?"

"We both worked on it at the end of last summer to get it ready for spring."

A spring Logan never saw...

It meant Cassie had done all the planting. "You've made the place beautiful."

"Thank you. Your father asked me to pick out some

porch furniture so it would look more attractive. When I was young I read all the books in the Little House series. I loved them and envied Laura Ingalls Wilder her life."

He wondered where she was going with this. "I remember watching a few TV shows based on those books."

Cassie flicked him a glance. "Do you know, when I first saw this place, I found myself thinking of it as *Little House in the Big Woods.* You know, it's isolated here. The forest is so pristine and untouched. Anyway, it gave me the same feeling as those books. I was really delighted when your father hired us to live and work here. It's an adorable house in the perfect setting."

Trace was charmed by her. "Well, with what you've done to it, it is now. Tell me—do you plan on writing a series of books about this house, too?"

"Don't be silly."

He eyed her very fetching profile. "You have a real talent for color and design. There are chalets in the Alps with shutters that can't touch the beauty of your artwork. Dad should have hired you years ago. How many other homes have you worked on?"

"None." She sounded surprised. "I'm not an artist, Trace. But a few years ago some of my college friends and I went on spring break to Europe. When we toured through Switzerland, I stayed in a village where all the chalets had decorated shutters and window boxes. I was so delighted by them, I took pictures and thought I'd like to try my hand if I ever got the chance. Your father, bless his heart, was willing to let me experiment."

"He got more than his money's worth. I'm very impressed." He was impressed with a lot of things about her. She was well traveled, could grow a garden and make jam, paint and was an expert horsewoman, as well. Trace had no doubts she could ride Masala if she wanted. He got the feeling she was holding something back where the horse was concerned, but he wasn't about to push his theory about why at this early stage.

"Tell me about your deployment in Italy. What was it like to be a jet pilot?"

His career seemed to be a safe topic for her, so he obliged her. "In a word, *exhilarating.*"

"But what was your job exactly?"

"The mission of the Thirty-First Fighter Wing is to deliver combat power and support across the globe to achieve U.S. and NATO objectives."

"I guess you had to memorize that for everyone who asks." He smiled at her perception.

"So what did you do when you weren't fighting?"

"We had to maintain aircraft and personnel in a high state of readiness. That involved a lot of training exercises."

"Did you get your eye injury in combat? I hope you don't mind my asking. When your father received the news, he was too broken up to talk about it."

So was Trace's girlfriend, Nicci. She'd begged him to go to work for her father so nothing between them would change. But everything *had* changed. There was no going back.

For their marriage to take place, she would have to move to Colorado. But she'd been living in denial since his injury and their relationship had hit a plateau.

Not so for the woman riding on the horse next to him. Unlike Nicoletta, Cassie had been forced to face losing her husband and get on with living and working. You couldn't avoid dealing with death. Her life couldn't get more real than that. Since she'd asked the question, why not tell her the truth?

"I was flying a combat mission when a laser beam intersected my eye. If you want the medical version, the light was transmitted through the clear ocular media and imaged onto a small spot on the sensory retina. In a mere moment tissue necrosis occurred. The result being that my vision was impaired."

"A laser? Where did it come from?"

"Lasers are used for different functions in military applications. They serve in targeting guidance systems. Some are fire-control devices, others for access denial systems and communications security. Although the use of lasers as a weapon is a violation of the Geneva convention, the potential for its wrongful use continues to attract international concern. The laser that injured my eye was no accident."

She shivered. "That's horrible. Evil."

"You're right. In military applications, just a few microjoules of laser through the pupils in a 10 to 30 nanosecond pulse can produce a visible lesion. At 150 to 300 microjoules, a small retinal hemorrhage can occur. This type of damage can have a devastating effect on a pilot's vision. It did on mine." His voice grated. "I wasn't blinded, but I have to wear a corrective lens so it prevents me from doing that particular job anymore."

"Though you're no longer top gun, you can still fly, right?"

"Yes. I could be a flight navigator, but once you've done what I do, no other position holds the same excitement for me. That probably sounds selfish to you."

"Not at all," she replied. "There are few careers in this world that demand your specialized kind of expertise. Connor and I had a talk about that very thing last week. Since his injury, his fans have been begging him to get back to steer wrestling and go for a sixth world championship title."

"What did he say?" Trace was curious.

"He admitted that those years of being on top were great, and there was no other thrill like it. But the injury affected him enough that he knew he'd never be that good again. Sure he could train and go for it over and over for a few more years, but he'd never be able to perform at his former level. To be a has-been simply wasn't for him.

"Then he gave me that special smile of his and told me he was glad he'd been injured because he ended up marrying Liz Henson. To quote him, 'The thrill of being married to her has topped anything I've ever experienced.'"

Trace liked hearing that. "He's really happy, then."

"Ecstatic. They both are. From the time we were in high school Liz had a crush on him that never went away."

He nodded. "Dad let on to me about her heartache before she and Connor traveled to Las Vegas together for the National Finals Rodeo. That trip turned their lives around and lost him a great vet in the process."

"It about killed her when he married Reva Stevens. I wasn't surprised when it ended in divorce so fast. Reva loved Connor, but she hated ranch life. Not everyone takes to it. She didn't last long. At the time I was afraid his heart was permanently broken."

"My mother couldn't handle being this isolated either," Trace admitted. "Nine years into the marriage and she asked my dad for a divorce." Would the same thing happen if he and Nicoletta got married, even if they lived in Colorado? He'd been struggling with that question all night.

"For someone who wasn't born to it, your mom lasted longer than most, Trace. That's because she loved your father. At least that's what I heard from people who knew your parents. But I know that's no consolation to you. Anything but. Forgive me for saying something so insensitive."

"There's nothing to forgive. I was the one to bring it up. My mother was frank with me. I knew she loved Dad, but that wasn't enough. I'm glad you told me about Connor. It's great to hear he's found his happiness now."

"I agree, but I'm so sorry about your injury, Trace. It isn't fair," she said in a heartfelt voice. "I'm surprised nothing's been done to prevent such a thing from happening."

"People have tried. There was an international conventional weapons conference in 1995. They announced the latest protocol on blinding laser weapons.

The United States signed on to the guidelines. Four of the articles outlined the parameters for the use of lasers in military maneuvers and war.

"They came up with the rule that the employment of lasers solely to cause permanent blindness—or a resulting visual acuity of 20/200—is strictly prohibited. But of course, the enemy doesn't care."

"That is so horrible."

"No more horrible than your husband being shot." Trace wanted to move the subject away from him. "Did the rangers find the person responsible?"

She was quiet for a moment before she admitted, "Not yet. As you know, Avery's husband, Zane, is a special agent for the Bureau of Land Management. While searching for Logan, he found a dead marten near Logan that had been shot on the property that day.

"The slug from a smooth bore shotgun that killed my husband matched the slug in the marten. Zane's still hoping forensics will lead to the owner of the shotgun so he can be brought in for questioning. So far there's no actual proof that it wasn't accidental."

"What do *you* think?"

"I don't know. There's no hunting until April, so whoever was out there in February was trespassing. It could have been an accident, but Zane doesn't think so. A hunter shooting marten would probably have taken it for the fur."

"Did your husband have an enemy?"

They'd come to the first stream running through the property. Both horses stopped to drink. "He was so likeable, I can't imagine it. But *I* have one." She sounded haunted.

"Who is it?"

"My brother Ned."

Chapter Two

Trace scowled. Through his father he knew all about Ned Bannock's instability. "Isn't he in a special mental facility in Billings?"

"He was, but has been getting treatment. In February the doctor allowed him to live at home for a month on a trial basis. According to my older married cousins, he was subdued and seemed to get along well enough. The doctor was pleased with his progress and said if he continued to improve, he'd be able to come home permanently."

"So he was at home during the time your husband was killed?"

"Yes. When he was first put in the facility, the court ordered our family to go into counseling and get therapy. It was painful, but necessary. I welcomed it because I knew that Ned had always resented me. There were times when I felt that he wished I weren't alive. I was able to express those feelings in front of my parents."

Since Trace didn't have a sibling, he couldn't relate, but her admission horrified him. "How did they react?"

"They were oblivious to my pain. Dad said I brought

on trouble, that when things went wrong with Ned it was my fault. Mom kept quiet to appease my dad, who claimed that I wasn't sensitive enough to Ned's needs growing up because I was the popular one. I should have included him more in my activities. Their worry over him meant more punishment for me if I didn't coddle my brother. To this day they still believe that. There's no getting through to them."

"I don't see how you've been able to cope. Under those conditions I probably would have run away."

"Once I was out of the house working on my own, I didn't have to be around him nearly as much. What stunned me was to learn in one of the sessions that Ned had hate issues with me because I'd gotten involved with Logan on one of my brief trips home."

"You're serious." Trace was appalled.

"I swear my brother was born a bigot. He felt that a hired hand wasn't good enough to be part of our family. Long before I told my parents I was in love with Logan, Ned had been filling my father with lies about him. Ned was the one who told my parents I was involved with him and it should be stopped."

"Sounds like he was driven by the same kind of hatred that landed Jarod in the hospital."

"Exactly. Dad, who was in a bad way at the time because of what Ned had tried to do to Jarod, wasn't thinking rationally. Like my older brothers, he'd always been afraid of Ned's temper and as usual took his side to placate him. He fired Logan and ordered me not to marry him in order to keep the peace."

"He *ordered* you?" Trace was incredulous.

"Dad used the very word. Shocking, isn't it? But I couldn't obey him. At that point he told me that if we went ahead with our marriage, then I no longer had a home with the family. Out of fear, Mother backed Dad by not saying anything at all. My other brothers took their cue from mom and stayed out of things."

Incredible. "I had no idea of the stress you've been through." And here Trace had been wondering why she hadn't gone home to her family after her husband was killed. She'd never want to go there again unless a miracle happened.

"No one knew. It isn't something you want other people to know, but I'm aware of your close friendship with my cousins and realize you probably know everything."

No, not everything. Not this.

She let out a deep sigh. "I loved Logan, so that was that. We got married in a civil ceremony and took a job with your father to run the ranch for him. I broke down and told him my whole situation. He's such a wonderful man. Mostly I checked hunting permits and collected fees while Logan monitored the hunters' activities throughout the season. Thanks to your dad, this job saved our lives."

So many people loved and respected Trace's father. He was an exceptional man. "I take it nothing has changed with your family?"

She hunched her shoulders. "Absolutely nothing. Though extended family and a lot of neighbors came to Logan's funeral in White Lodge, my parents didn't come near or even try to talk to me."

"I can't conceive of it. There's something very wrong with him, Cassie."

"I know. The doctor has urged me to stay in therapy. I'm glad I have because I've since learned that along with their other emotional problems, my parents are battered people and need a lot of intensive counseling."

"I could have used therapy when I was young," Trace admitted in a moment of self-reflection.

"Everyone could. In the case of our family I've learned that Ned irritated our older brothers to the point they didn't want to be around him. Ned had already felt abandoned when Sadie, the girl he'd always loved, married my cousin Jarod. In his jealousy he almost killed Jarod in order to get rid of him."

Trace nodded. "It was very tragic."

Cassie grimaced. "When I married Logan and moved away from the ranch, Ned began nursing an unhealthy hatred toward me."

"You think he could have killed your husband to hurt you?"

"It's possible," she said, "but I don't know how he could have left the ranch without someone knowing about it. Zane did an investigation. None of my father's firearms were missing or had been fired close to that time. In any event, Dad had people keeping an eye on my brother."

"But if he went off his meds, he might have found a way to make it over to this ranch. Is that what you're thinking?" Trace asked.

"He could have. One of the guys he hung around with in high school is still his friend and visits him.

Through him it's possible he got hold of a gun or rifle he hid somewhere before he'd been committed. I try not to think about it or I get ill."

"That's why the military disqualifies a person with a history of mood or behavioral disorders."

"Exactly. But home isn't the military, and my parents want him back to help around the ranch."

"That's hard on everyone."

"I've talked this over with Zane. If Ned was the one responsible, Zane will find out in time. After the shooting, he advised your father to close the ranch to hunting and keep it closed until more proof of what really happened came to light. As you know, he was a tough Navy SEAL before he started working as a special agent for the BLM."

"I know him by reputation. Let's hope he has an answer for you soon."

"Yes. Avery said Ned is going to be coming back to live with my parents again on a permanent basis." The anxiety in her eyes spoke volumes.

Trace cringed for her. "With restrictions, of course."

"I don't know what they'd be as long as he keeps taking his medicine."

"Cassie, I'm sorry you've had to live through such pain." To lose her husband and be afraid that her brother might have been the one to shoot him was horrendous. Worse, he could tell she was worried that Ned might come after her one day when he got the chance. That frightening possibility was going to keep Trace awake nights from here on out.

He couldn't begin to imagine the pain of Cassie's

loss, but she was obviously handling it. She was a strong woman to have married for love despite her father's wishes. Trace admired that strength and her will to get on with her life.

Just then his cell rang. He checked the caller ID. "It's my dad. He's on his way to the ranch now."

"Then let's get back. I have a pot roast with potatoes and carrots cooking."

"I could smell it before we left the house. Did he tell you that's my favorite meal?"

She smiled. "That's why I made it. To welcome you home. He's so happy you're going to be living here from now on, you can't imagine."

Trace was afraid he could and didn't look forward to the conversation he was about to have. When they reached the barn and dismounted to take care of the horses, he turned to her. She was removing Buttercup's bridle. "I want to thank you for what you and Logan have done."

"We were just doing our job."

"It was a lot more than that and you know it. You've eased my father's mind while I've been away and made the place beautiful. There's no way to repay you. I'll feed and water the horses while you go into the house. It's the least I can do."

Once dinner was over, Trace went out on the front porch with his father. He sat on a chair while his dad settled for the swing. "That Cassie could make her living as a cook."

"Agreed. I can't remember the last time I had a meal that good."

His dad studied Trace. "You're talking home cooked. Nothing like it." Trace nodded. "Do you have any idea how good it feels to be sitting on the porch with my son after all these years?"

Trace's throat thickened. "I do," he murmured. *More than you can imagine.*

His dad's hair was a sandy color mixed with gray. Lines from years of outdoor living gave his rugged features character. He'd dressed in one of his familiar plaid shirts and jeans, and he wore a belt with a silver and turquoise buckle, his trademark.

One of the tribal elders from the reservation had presented it to him for saving their horses from dying during an equine flu epidemic. The tribe had bought some horses in Mexico and had them transported. But several of them had the virus. Afraid all the horses would die, they came to Trace's father.

Trace, who had been only eight years old at the time, remembered going out to the reservation with him to test the horses. Sam told the elders all they could do was rest them for a month in fresh air in a shady, confined area. Walk them for short periods to maintain circulation during the fever and coughing. Keep them away from dust and hay to minimize the risk of bacterial infections of the lungs. Then give them an antibody vaccine booster every three months.

The horses looked and sounded miserable to Trace. He couldn't imagine his father's treatment working. But in a month's time the tribe hadn't lost one of them and he'd become a valued friend of the Crow.

Tears smarted Trace's eyes just remembering the

day they presented his dad with the belt buckle, hand-made on their reservation. His father was held in high esteem by a lot of the population around White Lodge, including members of the Crow nation.

Soon after that experience, his parents divorced. Remembered pain still lingered to think his mom would want to leave the man who was Trace's idol. So what did Trace do? After he'd turned eighteen, he'd left his father, just like his mom had done.

"You probably won't believe me, but I've missed being here. I've missed you, Dad." His voice was thick with emotion. "More than you'll ever know."

Sam leaned forward with his hands on his knees. "When your mom left, the heart went out of our home. You couldn't take it."

He shook his head. "That's not it. At first I was angry at her. Later I was angry at you for not making her come back."

"You can't hold somebody who doesn't want to be held, son."

"I know that now. Forgive my anger."

"It was natural. Divorce means an automatic whammy for everyone involved. No one escapes. I'm proud of you for what you've done with your life even when it threw you some curveballs. Is it killing you not to be a pilot anymore?"

"If you'd asked me that when I was rushed to the hospital, I would have told you I'd rather have been killed. But after a few days I realized it would be the coward's way out and I thought about something you said the day our collie's paw got caught in a snare and had to be amputated."

"Poor Kip. He was the best dog we ever had."

"I loved him. While I was having hysterics, you told me he'd be able to get around just fine with three legs. That's why God gave him four, just in case."

A quiet laugh came out of his father. "Did I really say that?"

"That's why everyone in Carbon County puts their favorite vet on a pedestal. Before I phoned you from the hospital to let you know what had happened to me, I figured you'd say something like, 'Son? God gave you two eyes so if you lost one of them, it didn't matter.' Even if you didn't know what went through my mind before our phone call, your wisdom helped me through that dark period. So, the answer to your question is no, it didn't kill me."

"Thank God for that."

"But during my recuperation I had to think about how else I could earn my living. On the way home, I spent a couple days at the Air Force Academy in Colorado Springs. They've offered me a teaching position on their staff, but I've been given five to six weeks to get my affairs in order before I report."

At that piece of unexpected news his dad—hurt to the marrow as Trace had anticipated—got up from the swing and walked over to the porch railing. He looked up at the stars. "What about the woman you said you wanted to marry in Italy? How does she feel about that decision?"

Trace couldn't stay seated either. He wandered over

to his father. "You're the smartest man I ever knew, so you already know the answer to that question."

"Which means *if* she's willing, you'll live in Colorado Springs."

The hollowness of his father's voice stung Trace. His eyes closed tightly for a minute. It was a big *if.*

"That's the plan, but these are early days. Nicci needs to fly to the States. I want her to meet you and Ellen, then we'll fly to Colorado Springs and let her get a feel for where we'd live."

Trace waited for the next question. It was a long time coming. "What about the ranch?"

This was the part he'd been dreading. "I'd like to use the time while I'm here to find a buyer. With the sale of the house and property, you'll have plenty of money to spend on you and Ellen.

"All these years you've sacrificed for me, for mom. Now it's time you thought about yourself. You can go on some cruises, buy a house. I was hoping you might invest in a motor home. Then you and Ellen could come and visit us in Colorado whenever you wanted."

His father slowly turned to him. In the semidarkness he looked older than he had earlier in the evening. "This ranch is your legacy, son."

Here Trace went again, stabbing his father in the heart once more. "Not when I won't be able to live here. Since you have health issues and can't work the ranch anymore, the only sensible thing to do is sell it. Maybe one of Ellen's married children would like to buy it."

His dad's body had gone still as a statue. "You know what? It's getting late. I don't want Ellen to worry, so

I'm going to leave. I've already said good-night to Cassie. But you tell her again how much I appreciated dinner."

He started for the porch steps. Trace walked with him to his truck. After he got in the cab, he lowered the window. "Didn't she do a great job on those shutters?"

The question only added to Trace's pain because he knew the renovations had been done expressly for Trace's homecoming. "They're exquisitely done."

His father nodded. "Come on over to the condo anytime. Don't be a stranger."

This wasn't the way their reunion was supposed to go. "What are you talking about? I'll see you tomorrow at the clinic. Love you, Dad."

"Love you. Always."

In agony, Trace watched his father drive away. If it weren't late, he'd head over to the Bannock ranch to look up Connor or Jarod. They'd understand his impossible position. Letting out a groan, he went back in the house for his wallet and keys. A restlessness had come over him. He'd never be able to sleep.

Cassie had already disappeared to her room for the night. Not wanting to disturb her, he left a note on the kitchen table that he was going into town and probably wouldn't be back till late. He supposed he didn't need to say anything, but it seemed the courteous thing to do. She'd gone the extra mile to make Trace comfortable today. No one had fussed over him like this in years and he appreciated it.

The Golden Spur Bar in White Lodge didn't close till one in the morning. He needed the canned country

music, a lot of noise plus a beer to drown the condemn-
ing voice in his head. Too bad the laser's damage hadn't
burned the guilt out of him at the same time.

He found a parking spot around the corner. Summer brought the tourists in droves and the place was
crowded. Trace made his way through to the bar. After
a five-minute wait he grabbed a vacated stool and sig-
naled the bartender.

"Trace Rafferty?" The man on his left had spoken to
him. When he turned, the guy said, "It *is* you. You're
the F-16 pilot. What do you know about that."

"Sorry. Have we met before?"

"Yeah, but it was a long time ago and I'm the forget-
table type according to my ex-wife. The name's Owen
Pearson."

It rang a bell, but Trace couldn't place him. Between
the empty whiskey glass and his self-pity, Trace could
see Owen was getting wasted fast. The bartender asked
Trace what he wanted. "A beer please."

Owen raised his empty glass. "Another one of these
while you're at it." Then his gaze swerved back to Trace.
"You in town on leave?"

"Something like that." It was no one else's business.

"Haven't figured it out yet, have you?"

"Pardon?"

"You remember Ned Bannock. He and I have been
buddies for years."

At the mention of the name, the hackles went up
on the back of Trace's neck. It all came back to him.
Owen Pearson was the one who lent Ned the truck that

had bashed Jarod's truck years ago almost killing him. "Your dad's ranch is right next door to the Bannock's."

The conversation with Cassie was still fresh in Trace's mind. His teeth snapped together. "That's right." Ned and Cassie's parents lived on the Bannock property owned by Ralph and Tyson Bannock, the two brothers who raised their families side by side.

"Then you'd know all about the shooting."

"My father filled me in. Did you go to the funeral?"

"Hell, no. Logan Dorney was a no-account. Ned's dad fired him when he found out he'd been doing Ned's sister on the sly. I'm surprised your dad hired them."

Sickness started to rise in Trace's throat. "That's my father's business surely."

"The Doc didn't know Logan the way Ned did."

Trace let the remark pass. "Any idea who shot him?"

"Some hunter."

Yup. "How is Ned these days? I haven't seen him in years."

"He had some family problems for a while. His sister was nothing but trouble for him. But he's doing much better now and will be home before long. We're going to go into business together soon."

"Is that right? What kind?"

"A stud farm for feral horses."

That was the business Connor had been building with Liz. "Where?"

"My dad's ranch."

The conversation robbed Trace of any interest in his beer. It was still sitting there untouched. He put some money on the counter and got to his feet.

"Hey—you haven't drunk your beer."

"I discovered I'm not thirsty. It's all yours. So long."

In a different frame of mind than before, Trace drove back to the ranch. After he reached the house, he tore up the note in the kitchen and wrote another one. She'd see it first thing in the morning.

Cassie—

I've gone to Billings and will be in and out of the house at odd hours for the rest of the week. Dad and I agree your food is out of this world, but please don't do any more cooking for me since I don't have a schedule you can count on.

T.

When Friday the twenty-second came around, Cassie kept her afternoon appointment with her OB. Dr. Raynard did an ultrasound and handed her the picture of the sonogram. "Your little girl has a healthy heart and measures the right size. So far everything looks fine."

Tears streamed down her cheeks. "I can't believe that's my baby. Oh, I wish Logan were here."

"Of course you do."

"You're sure she's all right?"

"Yes, but to make certain she stays that way, I'm going to insist you stop your horseback riding altogether."

"Since my last appointment I've stopped riding Masala, but Buttercup is gentle. I love riding so much."

"At twenty weeks, you're too far along to take any chances. That isn't a great deal to give up. Go on walks instead."

"Okay. I haven't felt the baby move yet. How come?"

"It's been moving for a long time, but too small for you to notice. I imagine you'll feel it within the next couple of weeks."

"I hope so."

"And I hope you mind me. I know you're an expert rider, but a horse can do the unexpected. Do you hear what I'm saying? This is for your own good. If your husband were alive, he wouldn't want you to ride now."

"Probably not."

He smiled. "I'll see you in a month. That'll make it Friday, July 22. Remember to go easy on salt and caffeine, and put your legs up for a few minutes every day."

"I will. Thanks so much."

Cassie left the White Lodge Clinic where Dr. Raynard practiced and did a little shopping. She couldn't hide her pregnancy any longer. She needed to buy another couple of pairs of maternity pants and a few more tops she could layer. Now that she knew she was having a daughter, she would pick up a few things for the baby at the same time.

When Logan was killed, Cassie hadn't known she was pregnant. Later she became ill and went to see the doctor because she'd thought she'd come down with the flu. The news that she was pregnant had sent her into shock again, but a wonderful kind. A part of Logan was growing inside her.

To know she had their baby to live for pulled her out

of the dark depression she'd been in. The doctor gave her medicine to help with the morning sickness. Since that stage had passed, she'd never felt better.

Later tonight she would drive over to Zane's ranch and show Avery the new things she'd bought for the baby while they talked. Avery was the closest thing she had to a sister. Her cousin was the only one who knew she was pregnant, but Cassie wouldn't be able to keep it a secret from now on.

When she returned to the ranch, there was still no sign of Trace. No doubt he was spending a lot of time with his father in town. She hurried inside to change into her new clothes that gave her more room to breathe. After grabbing a sandwich, she went out to the barn to take the horses for a late afternoon walk, mindful of her doctor's advice.

"Come on, Buttercup. You first."

If her horse thought it strange Cassie didn't mount her, Cassie would never know. She walked her as far as the stream, then left her to graze in the paddock. It was Masala's turn next. He was used to trailing behind her. When they returned to the paddock, Masala joined Buttercup. To Cassie's amusement, her horse moved her head against his neck.

"I think you two like each other!" she exclaimed. "Liz said it could happen, but I can't believe it!"

"So I wasn't wrong," spoke a deep male voice right behind her. She spun around in surprise and discovered Trace's blue eyes eyeing her as if he could see right through her. A rush of warmth enveloped her.

"I didn't know you were home," she said, out of

breath for no good reason. She'd begun to think he was never coming back. It surprised her how much pleasure she felt at seeing him.

"I got here a little while ago."

"You've been making yourself scarce."

"I'm back for the weekend. When I looked out the kitchen window and saw that you weren't riding Buttercup, I wondered if my first suspicions about you were correct. Now I know."

Her heart fluttered like the wings of a darning needle she could see flitting around. "First suspicions about what?"

"That you're pregnant. When you told me Masala wasn't your horse, I wondered if pregnancy was the reason you wouldn't ride him. You've hidden your pregnancy so well, no one would suspect."

"*You* did, though," she remarked.

"Well, that's because we went riding on Tuesday and I was close enough to you to notice. Does my dad know?"

She averted her eyes. "No one does except my doctor and Avery. But your dad is a doctor who has delivered a lot of foals. He has probably guessed. I'm quite sure it's the reason he's let me stay on here without saying anything. He's such an understanding man. You can't hide much from him."

His eyes smiled. "Nope." He cocked his head. "I don't mean to pry, but why have you kept it a secret?"

"Because I'm trying to make my way on my own. My parents never forgave me for marrying Logan. Once they find out I'm having his baby—and they will—they'll write my child off completely, too."

"But you're carrying their grandchild!"

"They don't want one from a lowlife like Logan. That's what Ned called my husband because Logan was an orphan. In my family, if you don't have a pedigree dating back to the turn of the last century, you're not acceptable."

A grimace marred his handsome features. "Your brother's a sick man."

"I know. Ned had no idea how much I loved Logan. Neither did my parents. It's their loss now." She was all fired up at this point. "I intend to prove that I'm independent and will make a good mother even if it kills me—"

"I'm already convinced nothing could do that."

She let out a laugh. "Sorry I got so heated."

"It's understandable. When are you due?"

"October 14."

"You must be about five months along. Do you know the gender?"

Cassie nodded. "I found out today."

His lips twitched. "Are you planning to keep me in suspense?"

"I'm going to have a girl. I bought some baby clothes for her in town after my doctor's appointment. He gave me a picture of the sonogram."

"I've never seen one. You'll have to show it to me."

"As it happens, I have it right here because I can't stop looking at it." She reached in her jeans pocket and pulled it out. He moved next to her so they could look at it together.

"That's incredible," he said in a husky voice.

"I know. While he took the picture, her heartbeat was so strong and loud, it made everything real for the first time."

"Did you and Logan pick out names for the baby before he died?"

Cassie put the picture back in her pocket. "I didn't learn I was pregnant until a few weeks after his death."

"That's tough. I'm sorry," he murmured. "You really are doing this on your own."

"It's all right. Finding out I was pregnant gave me a whole new lease on life."

"You're a remarkable woman, Cassie."

Her eyes met his searching gaze. "Say that to me when I'm old and have raised a terrific daughter, and I'll believe you." Surprised they'd spent this long talking she said, "I've got to go in and finish putting up the strawberries I picked this morning." She would prepare a meatloaf and potatoes to go in the oven at the same time.

"While you do that, I'll take the horses back to the barn and settle them in."

They weren't his responsibility, but there was no point in fighting him on it. "That would be great. Thank you."

Much as she appreciated Trace's help, she felt guilty. Now that he knew she was pregnant, it changed everything. Cassie could tell he had a protective streak in him like his father. She didn't want him treating her any differently, but it was too late because he'd already figured it out just by looking at her blossoming figure.

Trying not to think about how excited he'd sounded when he'd looked at the baby picture, she prepared the dinner, then continued to make jam. Her raspberries would be coming into season soon. White Lodge had a fair in the fall. She could sell her wares and hopefully make enough money to buy a crib and the basic items she'd need for the baby.

Trace had asked her about a name. She didn't know yet, but the fact that he'd asked told her he was a caring, sensitive man. Cassie was thinking too much about him. What on earth was wrong with her?

While she was pouring the hot paraffin wax over the filled jars to seal them, she heard him come in the back door. He didn't pause to talk so she didn't say anything. *Forget he's here, Cassie.*

Chapter Three

Trace walked down the hall. The meeting with the therapist in Billings earlier today had gone as he'd imagined. He didn't need a doctor to realize he'd been in a morose state since his eye injury. It was all part of his PTSD. But Dr. Holbrook had emphasized that there was one thing he needed to do before all else. Deal with Nicci. No other decision should be made until he knew if he was going to live in Colorado or Italy.

The therapist made a lot of sense. It was time for a heart-to-heart.

Now that Trace was on the ranch and had spent two full days with his father, it was time to pay Nicci some attention. A month had passed since he'd last seen her. They'd spoken several times since, but nothing had been resolved. His call to her yesterday had gone downhill. They needed to talk when her father wasn't around.

She picked up on the fifth ring. *"Caro—"* she answered in a sleepy voice.

"Nicci? Sorry for calling you in the middle of the night, but this can't wait. Our conversation yesterday wasn't good."

"That's because I'm miserable," she said in heavily accented English. "Papa wants to know if you have come to your senses yet. Please say yes. Is that why you're phoning while I was dreaming about the two of us in our own villa overlooking the water?"

Clearly nothing in her mind had changed since he'd left Italy. His eyes closed tightly. "I can't say yes. All I know is that I miss you."

"I think not enough, or you would take the job my father has offered you. I never knew anyone so obstinate." That was her temper talking because she was in pain. So was he.

Trace paced the floor. "Listen to me, Nicci. I have to use my expertise. As I told you, the Air Force Academy has offered me a position as a flight instructor. Colorado Springs is a beautiful city. You'll love it there. We'll buy a house and start a family. You'll be able to visit your family often. They'll visit us. We'll visit my father and his wife. They'll come to us. We can have the life we wanted."

The silence on the other end was tangible. "But it's *not* the life we planned."

"Only the location and the kind of work I do have changed. *We* haven't."

"I don't know. What would I do all day while you're at work?"

"We talked about that yesterday. You can find a job here you like. I have contacts."

"But it won't be like helping Papa."

"Of course nothing would be like that, Nicci." She was his social princess and did things for him only a daughter could do, but you could never call it a job. Even Nicci was honest enough to admit that. He turned on his other side. Naturally he couldn't blame her for her fears, but the conversation was unraveling fast.

"You won't know how you feel until you try. When can you fly over?"

"I'm not sure."

He was used to her pouts, but since he'd been to the therapist he was more immune to them now. "This is hard on me, too, Nicci. Plan a time and I'll meet your plane in Denver. We'll drive to Colorado Springs so you can get a feel for it. We'll look at houses and plan. Then we'll fly to Montana so you can meet my father and his wife. What do you say?"

"I say I miss you so much, I feel like I'm going mad."

He could just picture her stomping the floor in one of her spiky high heels. Trace wouldn't be getting a definitive answer out of her yet. Maybe never. "I love you, too. Phone me when you've picked the date to fly over."

"What are you going to do now?"

"Eat dinner and go to bed. It's been a long day and I'm exhausted." But that exhaustion was of the mental kind.

"That's where I wish we were right now."

He inhaled sharply. They'd always communicated well in bed. "Then hurry and make arrangements. I'll pay for your ticket."

"Papa will do it!"

"You know how I feel about that. I plan to take care of you."

"We're not married yet. He can afford it."

Yes he could. Benito Tornielli, who owned a company that constructed some of the largest cruise ships on the Adriatic, was a multimillionaire who spoiled his children. Trace almost said she would need to get used to living on his salary, but he caught himself in time.

She was so headstrong in favor of spending her father's money, this was one fight he couldn't win over the phone so there was no point in trying.

"Good night, Nicci. Come to me soon."

After they hung up, he lay back staring at the ceiling. Nicci still wasn't ready to fly over, which made their conversation more troubling to him than ever. She was a fiery, exciting woman who'd been pampered all her life and felt perfectly safe in her sheltered environment.

The accident that had changed his life had shaken her to the core. To live with him in Colorado away from her family was so frightening to her, she couldn't face it.

He understood. This would ask a lot of any woman from another country. But Nicci wasn't just any woman. The more he thought about it, the more he feared that marriage to her wouldn't work unless it was on her terms, which meant living in Italy.

For her sake he'd been wrestling with the idea of being a flight navigator since his injury. But enough time had passed during his recuperation that he knew in his heart it wasn't what he wanted. He'd expressed that sentiment to Cassie on Tuesday, and to the therapist today. He couldn't do that job, not even for love. Trace had to be true to himself. His father had taught him that much.

To work for Nicci's father—to be under his thumb

for the rest of their lives—was out of the question. So until she came to the United States to see if they could make a new life here work, then a marriage between them wasn't possible. She needed to be true to herself, too. Knowing his own mind helped him to deal with matters closer to home.

Trace left the bedroom and walked out to the kitchen to wash his hands. Cassie eyed him. "I was just going to call you to dinner."

His gaze darted to the table. She'd fixed him a plate of meatloaf and potatoes, but it looked like she was ready to disappear. "Since you've gone to so much trouble, why don't you eat with me?" It upset him that she felt she had to stay away when he was home for the evening.

"I can't. I have plans. Just leave everything when you've finished and I'll be back to do the dishes."

An unaccountable feeling of disappointment passed through him as she walked out the front door. He'd looked forward to talking to her. More important however, there was something he needed to discuss with her tonight. After his therapy session he realized it couldn't be put off.

His plans to sell the ranch had made her circumstances more precarious because she was pregnant. He hated the idea of bringing her added distress, but she needed to know his plans so she could think about making other work and living arrangements.

When he'd finished eating, he cleaned up the kitchen. Still at a loose end, he went to the bedroom for his laptop. After going to the living room, he looked up some real estate websites for Billings. From the long list, one name stood out he recognized. Over the years he'd seen Hawksworth Realty signs around the White Lodge area and figured they must be a reputable company.

While he jotted down the phone number, he heard the front door open and turned his head. The sight of Cassie brought him more pleasure than it should have. "Home so soon? You weren't gone long."

"No. I went to Avery's to show her the new baby clothes, but she and Zane weren't there so I came home."

"I'm glad you're back early. Since it's Friday night and not time for bed, would you like to drive into White Lodge and see a movie with me? I haven't done it in years. It might be fun." He'd broach the serious subject later.

She gave him a speculative glance. "This must be hard for you."

"What do you mean?"

"Being back here twiddling your thumbs after the life you spent overseas. Don't tell me there isn't a woman you left behind. Some time ago your father mentioned a particular woman you were crazy about. Do you still feel the same way about her?"

"You don't miss much, do you, Cassie."

Her eyes smiled. "It's not hard to pick up on the news when your dad talks about you all the time." At this point Trace's guilt weighed heavily on him. "What's her name?"

"Nicoletta Tornielli. I call her Nicci."

"I love that name. Italian and gorgeous?"

"As a matter of fact she is. Before my injury we were planning to get married and live in Italy. Now I'm afraid everything is on hold."

"Why?"

"Because I'll be working in Colorado."

"If she loves you, she'll go where you go."

"You don't know Nicci. She comes from a privileged background."

"Logan accused me of being privileged. He didn't believe I would leave my family to marry him and work here with him, but I did."

"But your family lives on the ranch next door."

Her features closed up. "As you know, they might as well be in Italy since my marriage to Logan."

"I forgot. That was insensitive of me."

She smiled. "Then we're even. What kind of work does she do?"

"Nicci waits on her father, but she doesn't work in the sense you mean by drawing a paycheck."

"What does he do?"

"His company builds ships that travel the Adriatic. He owns a huge villa and estate in Monfalcone overlooking the water."

"Um, that sounds fabulous."

"It is. I'm afraid Colorado Springs won't be able to compete."

"Has she been here before?"

"Only New York. I'm expecting her to fly over next week so I can show her around. But I'm not holding my breath. My instincts tell me she knows she won't transplant well."

"Give her a little more time."

He shook his head. "In her case I don't think time is going to make a difference."

Cassie's eyes filled with concern. "When you're in love, even a week sounds more like an eternity." After a pause, "If you want to see a movie tonight, I'd be happy to go."

Her comment pleased him no end. "So you're taking pity on me?"

"Why not? I could do with some diversion myself."

"You deserve it. We'll celebrate the news that you're expecting a daughter."

That brought a radiant smile to her face. She really was a beautiful woman. "I am! I can hardly believe it."

"You're not too tired?"

"Not yet."

"We'll go in my new car. You'll be the first person to ride in it."

"That sounds exciting. Do you know what's playing? All the years you've been away there are still only two movie theaters in our little hamlet."

He chuckled. "I remember, and I checked earlier. *The Amazing Spider-Man 2* or *Draft Day*."

"I've heard about the second option. I like a good football story. Let's go with that one."

So far there wasn't anything about Cassie Dorney he didn't like. "You're on."

"I'll meet you outside in a minute."

He waited for her on the porch steps to help her to his car. On the way to town she said, "You didn't need to do the dishes. I would have done them."

"I think I can handle putting a plate and glass in the dishwasher." A chuckle came out of her. "The meatloaf was so good I'm afraid I ate all that you cooked."

"You must have been starving."

"Since coming home I've noticed my normal appetite is back."

"That's good to hear. Your father was so worried while you were in the hospital."

"Sounds like you and Dad have gotten close."

"He's been a wonderful friend to Logan and me. I—" She stopped talking.

"I know what you were going to say, Cassie. How could I have chosen a career that kept me away from him all these years?"

"No. I was just going to say that you were lucky to have been raised by a father who loves you so completely."

The situation with Cassie and her father was tragic. "I wish my anger over the divorce hadn't carried me down a path of separation for as long as it did." The laser injury dictated more separation, but not as far away from home as before.

They drove into White Lodge. Summer tourists had invaded the place. When he'd parked and they'd walked to the theater, he discovered it was packed. They were lucky to get seats on the next to the last row. Cassie refused the popcorn Trace bought them. "I'd love some, but the doctor told me to watch my salt intake and put my feet up every day for a while."

"I'll remember that and we'll bring our own unsalted version next time."

THERE WOULDN'T BE a next time, but Cassie didn't say anything. The woman he planned to marry would be here before long. Cassie couldn't imagine his girlfriend letting him get away from her. It was just his depression talking.

After he'd helped her down from his elegant new Explorer, he'd cupped her elbow as they'd walked to the movie theatre. Because she was pregnant and wearing maternity clothes that showed her bump, people no doubt thought they were a married couple. If anyone recognized her, word would get back to her family, but it had to happen sometime. She couldn't worry about it now.

This was the first time Cassie had been anywhere with another man since Logan. Oddly enough she didn't feel uncomfortable, probably because Trace wasn't just another man. He was Sam Rafferty's son. Cassie had known them since she was a young girl.

She and Trace had already confided in each other over the traumas in their lives. The unconventional situation of them being thrown together had forced secrets to be divulged, putting them on a more intimate footing.

Most of the females who saw her with Trace couldn't take their eyes off him. Even before he'd arrived at the ranch, Avery and Liz had commented that he was one of the most attractive men they'd ever seen in their lives, but they'd said it out of earshot of their husbands.

Cassie agreed with them. Endowed with dark hair and those blazing blue eyes, Trace turned heads, especially in his black cowboy hat. He looked the part, but she'd seen the pictures of him in uniform. He looked the part of a pilot, too. With his intelligence and charisma, he could be anything he wanted.

His Italian girlfriend was lucky to be loved by a

man like him. Nicci was so blessed that Trace was still alive, but until tragedy happened, you couldn't appreciate what you had. Tears smarted Cassie's eyes. She blinked them away, disturbed by a tumult of emotions attacking her.

It hadn't been a good idea to come out with Trace tonight after all. She'd been giving way too much thought to his life and situation. Worse, she felt guilty that she was enjoying herself. Logan had only been gone half a year. To her chagrin she sensed an attraction to Trace deep down she couldn't explain. It was starting to disturb her.

She could blame it on hormones or the fact that she was a widow. Cassie could blame it on whatever she wanted, but the fact still remained she found Trace appealing. On the walk to the theater she'd become aware of his touch. Sitting next to him in the dark, she could hear him breathe and discovered herself listening for his deep laugh. She smelled the soap he'd used in the shower. It was all too much.

How could this be happening to her? She was pregnant with her husband's child, and Trace was planning to marry another woman in the near future. Why was she so susceptible to him? Maybe she would feel this way around any attractive man now that Logan was gone. All Cassie knew was that at this point she needed to stay away from him whenever possible until he left for Colorado.

"Hey, Cassie?" A married friend who worked at the saddlery shop called to her as they left the theater.

"Hi, Mandy!"

The other woman, always cheerful, headed toward them. She was yet another female who'd seen Trace and couldn't resist. Cassie was forced to introduce him to her.

"You're Doc Rafferty's famous ace son!"

"Is that what I am?" His eyes danced, but he'd directed his question to Cassie, not Mandy. This shouldn't be happening either. Cassie was sure he didn't mean to, but he was behaving as if they were a couple. It gave the wrong impression. No, no, no.

Mandy smiled. "Modest, too." She whispered to Cassie. "I didn't know you were pregnant."

"I only found out after Logan died."

"Oh, wow. You've really been through it, but I'm so happy about your baby."

"So am I. It's a great blessing."

"Of course. You look terrific." She turned to Trace. "See you around, hotshot."

His male laughter followed behind Cassie as she hurried over to the Explorer. She would have climbed in without his help, but he'd locked it so she had to wait until he'd activated the remote. Though she didn't want his assistance, he helped her in anyway, then walked around and got in behind the wheel.

"At least she didn't call you Maverick," Cassie quipped to ease the effect his nearness had on her. "You know, the pilot in the film *Top Gun*. I'm afraid you're in for it because everyone knows your dad. You're all he ever talks about."

"I'm a legend before my time. Is that what you're saying?"

"Something like that."

"My father's the legend. Unfortunately I'm his greatest disappointment, but he's done his best not to let it show in public." Since Cassie knew how her dad felt about her, who was she to tell Trace how wrong he was if that was his perception. "Would you like to stop at the drive-thru for something?"

"Sure. A lemonade sounds good to me. Thanks."

They stopped long enough for drinks, then headed back to the ranch.

"Tell me something, Cassie. If Logan hadn't died, what were your plans for the future?"

She let out a deep sigh. "To make enough money to buy ourselves a modest little ranch somewhere in the Pryors where the horseback riding and fishing is good. Maybe run a head of cattle. And of course raise a family. It was a lovely dream while it lasted."

Once they reached the house, she got out before he could help her and hurried to unlock the front door. He was right behind her. "Thanks for the fun evening," she said without looking at him. "I really enjoyed it."

"So did I."

"See you in the morning."

"Cassie?"

She paused in her tracks and looked back at him. "Yes?"

He acted as if he was on the verge of saying something important, then apparently changed his mind. She discovered his eyes playing over her with disturbing intensity. "Please don't worry about getting my breakfast or dinner tomorrow. After I exercise the horses, I'll be out all day."

"All right. See you later, then."

Since Cassie knew he'd lock up and turn out the lights, she went straight to her bedroom. After being with him tonight, she realized how difficult it would be to live in the same house with Trace. It was a good thing he would be leaving for Colorado soon. She was conscious of his presence whenever he came near her. Mandy had already seen her with Trace and would be speculating on their relationship. It didn't look right and didn't feel right.

No more jaunts out in public with him. When she'd made the decision to go to the movie, she'd been trying to cheer him up. And honestly she was glad to get out and away from her loneliness for a little while. But her good intentions had backfired. Bumping into Mandy had been a wake-up call for her. Sam had hired her to keep up the house, not to entertain his son.

SATURDAY MORNING TRACE took Buttercup for a ride. After leaving her in the paddock, he put a bridle on Masala, whose ears pricked when he heard Trace coming. "Good news, big fella. We're going for a ride." He gentled him before putting on the bridle.

"It'll be your turn again tomorrow, Buttercup." Cassie's horse nickered, causing him to smile as he mounted Masala and they took off for the Bannock ranch. It had been a year at least since he'd been over there. Not only was he eager to see the Bannock brothers again, Trace was anxious to talk to them about the sale of the ranch. Following that conversation he needed to express his concerns about Cassie and what would happen to her when he sold the property.

Maybe Connor, his friend who'd become a legend as the world's greatest steer wrestling champion, knew someone in the region who'd like to buy the ranch. But when he reached the big corral on their property, it was Jarod he saw ride up in his truck.

The second he laid eyes on Trace, he got out of the cab and started toward him with a smile. Trace, in turn, jumped off Masala and tied him to the fencing before they gave each other a bear hug.

"Welcome home, Trace. We heard from your father that you were coming. You've been missed around here. Those visits home over the years weren't long or often enough."

"I agree. It's good to see you." He eyed Connor's older brother, whose long black hair tied back with a thong emphasized his half Apsáalooke heritage. "You look like fatherhood agrees with you."

"Sadie and I have never been happier." Those black eyes studied Trace for a moment. "You'd never know you suffered an eye injury as serious as yours. I'm sorry about what happened to you."

"It's life. When you go in the military, you take a risk."

They stared at each other before Jarod said, "Life's a risk under any circumstances as we've all found out."

"No question about it. How's Ralph?"

"Would you believe our grandfather is stronger and happier than I've seen him in years? He'll want to see you."

"I promise to stop by and visit him soon."

"Good. In the meantime come on over to our new house and meet our son Cole. Between him and Sadie's half brother Ryan, they've put fresh life into him."

"I'd love to, but I need to talk to you and Connor about a couple of things in private first." He was worried about Cassie for several reasons and wanted their input. Three heads were better than one.

"Connor will hate missing you, but he's up at the wild horse refuge office and probably won't be back till dinner."

"I knew it would be too much to hope for that you'd both be around at the same time, but I'll catch up with him later."

"What's on your mind, Trace?"

"Sure you have time?"

"For you, I'll always make time."

"Ditto."

Trace looked around to be certain they were out of earshot of the ranch hands. "You and Connor have known my situation from the beginning. Dad has sacrificed his whole life for me. Now I have a chance to pay him back. I'm only going to be home long enough to sell the ranch. He deserves to buy himself and Ellen a house they'd both love. With the money from the sale, they can have whatever they want. Their condo is too small and confining."

Jarod stood there with his arms folded. "I hear you. Where are *you* going?"

"Colorado Springs. I've accepted a position as a flight instructor at the academy."

His friend nodded without saying anything. Because of the partly stoic side of Jarod's nature, at times it was hard to read what was going on inside him.

"I'm afraid Dad didn't take the news well."

"He wouldn't. You're the bright spot in his life."

"Unfortunately I don't have a choice since I have to work at something I know. I'm expecting my Italian girlfriend Nicoletta to be flying over shortly. Before my eye injury, we were planning to be married and live in Italy. Now she's got to find out if she can adapt to living in Colorado before we make plans. As you can see, everything's up in the air."

Jarod had that faraway look in his eyes. "There was a time when I came to a crossroads after my accident and had to face difficult decisions. Sadie had fled to California to be with her mother. It felt like my life was over. My uncle Charlo knew my thoughts and warned me to think outward to seven generations before making any new plans."

You couldn't resent Jarod's words. There was wisdom in everything he said. Raffertys had only been here for four generations. According to Jarod's counsel, there were three more to go, taking him beyond his life span. Trace knew what his friend was saying, but he couldn't see another way out.

"Your uncle gives excellent advice."

"But hard to swallow. I know all about it." By the thick tone in Jarod's voice, Trace knew Jarod had been through years of torture before Sadie came back to him. "Have you forgotten you were a cowboy long before you became a pilot?"

Trace took a deep breath. "Life is different now. Dad will be doing vet work until he keels over, but with his arthritis he shouldn't have to worry about the ranch anymore. The problem is, I can't take care of things long distance when my future isn't here. Before I contact a Realtor, I'm wondering if you know anyone around here who might be interested in buying it."

Jarod took his time answering. "Your great-great-grandfather Rafferty picked out that prime piece of land to settle down for a reason." Guilt swamped Trace at the reminder, but circumstances were forcing him to sell. "Once the news is out, you'll be besieged with offers."

"That's what I'm hoping, but since our land borders yours, I want the right person living next door to you. I'd like to use you and Connor for a filter."

After a long silence Jarod said, "The right person is already living there."

Trace knew what he meant. "I appreciate those words, Jarod, but if Nicci can be happy with us living in Colorado, then that's what I need to do for both our sakes. Which brings me to my next concern. I didn't realize until I got home that Cassie was still living on the ranch taking care of the house since Logan's death. Somehow I'd taken it for granted she'd gone back to her parents' house. Since she didn't, this will mean a move for her which I hate to do to her considering the fact that she can't go home."

Lines darkened his face. "She wouldn't want to even if she were allowed."

"I know," Trace muttered. "She confided a lot to me yesterday."

His black eyes narrowed. "Does she know about your plans to sell the property?"

"No. I told her I'll be going to work in Colorado, but I've said nothing to her about finding a buyer for the ranch. As far as she knows, she's doing the job Dad hired her to do, which she's doing admirably well I might add."

"I'm glad you haven't told her yet. Cassie has always been a hard worker and I know she thrives on keeping the place up for Sam. But *I'm* not happy to learn you're selling the ranch. Connor won't be either." Jarod had always had a stubborn streak when he felt strongly about something. In ten years that hadn't changed.

"I don't see another way to handle this, and I'm worried about something else. I guess you know she's pregnant."

"I've had my suspicions, but you've just verified them."

"Then you understand my concern. Cassie intimated that Ned will be coming back to live with her parents one of these days. I saw fear in her eyes. She told me about the problems with her parents and the suspicious circumstances of the shooting during Ned's last visit home. I've been horrified by the things she told me."

His friend grimaced. "We're all worried about Ned, but I don't imagine he'll be allowed home for quite a while yet."

"Then you need to hear the news I got from the horse's mouth last night."

Jarod looked surprised. "About Ned?"

For the next few minutes Trace told him about the encounter with Owen Pearson at the Golden Spur. "He'd already had too much to drink when I got there. Everything that came out of his mouth verified Cassie's conviction that her brother hates her and hated Logan. According to Owen, Ned is going to be coming home any day now for good."

"That could be Ned's wishful thinking talking. But if it's true, then we're all in for a new nightmare sooner than we thought."

"There's more. Owen says they're going into the feral stud farm business on his father's ranch."

Jarod's features hardened. "So now he wants to compete with Connor? His jealousy is over the top, always has been. It'll never happen, Trace. That's another pipe dream of Ned's. Uncle Grant wants his son working around here, but Ned gets out of work any way he can. As for Owen, he's been in so much trouble because of Ned, his father would never allow it."

"He told me he's divorced."

"Yup. His short-lived marriage was another mistake. He keeps making them, and sticking like glue to Ned isn't helping. Zane needs to hear all this from you, but it's Saturday, which is his day to go out to the reservation with Avery. They probably won't be home until late."

"I'll try to get together with him tomorrow."

"Sunday will be a good time to find him home. Trace—do me a favor? Until you've talked to Zane, don't breathe a word of your plans to anyone about selling the ranch, especially not to Cassie. For reasons you don't know about, he'll want to hear everything you told me first."

That sounded cryptic. "Except to explain the situation to my father, I won't say anything. But I'm anxious for the opportunity to talk to Zane about Logan's death. Once Ned is home again, whenever that happens, I'm afraid Cassie could be in danger."

"My thoughts exactly."

"Don't let me keep you, Jarod. After I take Masala back, I need to drive into town and discuss Cassie's situation with Dad."

"Let's exchange phone numbers so we can stay in close touch."

"Good idea."

Chapter Four

Cassie left the house wearing a clean, pale green smock over her clothes and got in her truck. Every Saturday she volunteered at the White Lodge Wildlife Sanctuary. It was one of several public refuges in Montana to save animals that were too sick or injured to be returned to the wild, or were too humanized to survive there.

Today she was going to join her married friends Paul and Lindsey Shaw, also volunteers, to paint the railings in front of the outdoor wolf enclosures. The sanctuary was adding new sections to accommodate the animals and birds found struggling. If they recovered and could handle it, they'd be released to live in their former habitat. Otherwise they were well taken care of.

Every Saturday there was a different assignment to tackle. Cassie had been helping out for close to a year. More and more tourists stopped to see the wildlife. She could understand why. She loved the animals, too, and through perseverance had made friends of some of them.

As Cassie started the engine and backed up, Trace, wearing boots and Stetson, rode into her line of vision on Masala. She put on the brakes. Like his father, he was such a natural on a horse you'd never have guessed he was also an ace pilot whose career had been cut short.

Her pulse raced when the hard-muscled male astride the horse walked them right up to her open window. She was almost blinded by the intensity of his hot blue eyes. "Where are you going in such a hurry?"

"To the White Lodge Wildlife Sanctuary."

"I've heard of it, but have never seen it."

"You'd love it. I'd tell you more about it, but I volunteer there and I'm late. Have a nice day, Trace."

Without waiting for his response she took off down the dirt road. Seeing him had changed the rhythm of her heart. Until now she'd managed to put him out of her mind for a little while. It was astonishing how fast everything changed the minute he came near.

She was determined not to let him affect her day. Once she'd reached the area of the sanctuary closed off to tourists during renovation, she started painting with a vengeance.

Today's project happened right outside the fencing where the wolves were enclosed. Paul had been sanding the surfaces of the railings, so the paint went on evenly. The old structures were being refurbished. The brown color was a great improvement over the weathered wood that had never seen a coat of paint.

One of the gray she-wolves came up to the fence and howled at Cassie when she got to work.

"Don't be upset, Lulu. I know the smell is a hundred times stronger for you than for me, but it won't hurt you.

We'll be gone pretty soon." The minutes turned into a couple of hours.

Lindsey was painting the last railing. "Can you believe that constant yipping? It's coming from Annie who went into her house to get away from Paul. She hasn't stopped."

Cassie nodded. "Lulu is defending her. The sound of the sander frightens them. I didn't realize our work would stress them out so much. They're usually so calm. We'll be gone in a few more minutes, Lulu. Don't worry."

"Can anyone help?" spoke a deep, familiar male voice behind Cassie.

She turned around with brush in hand and almost dropped it. The man she'd been trying her hardest not to think about had come to the sanctuary. "Hi! What are you doing here?"

"I dropped by my Dad's for a while and thought I'd check out the sanctuary before heading back to the ranch. What's wrong with these wolves? They look healthy."

"They are now, thanks to your dad. Two winters ago someone found them near dead in the forest just outside the town. Sam tested them for mange. Mites had burrowed under their skin and the scratching caused so much hair loss, they almost froze to death. Unfortunately they're too domesticated now, so they have a permanent home here."

"Did he name them?"

"No. That was the owner of the sanctuary. She passed away a year ago at the age of ninety-five. I heard she loved the Little Lulu comic books as a child so she named these sister wolves Lulu and Annie. Aren't they beautiful?"

"They are," he murmured, but he was looking at her. She could hardly breathe.

"We're finished with the painting for today."

"I bet your OB would tell you not to get around paint."

"It's okay. We're outside, and this paint is VOC proofed. As long as you're here, you need to see my favorite animal. Let me put my things away first." She put the brush in the can of turpentine and sealed the paint can. As she started to pick them up, Trace took them from her and carried them down to the box at the end of the railing for her.

"Thank you," she said. "See you next week, guys," she called to her friends.

They waved her off.

"You won't believe how darling this little female fox is. Logan found her in the forest behind your house. He said she acted disoriented, so we took her to your dad's clinic. He discovered the poor darling was close to blind. Wait till you see her."

Trace followed her around to the next enclosure. "Right now she's housed in a special raptor mew waiting for new animal quarters. The owners call it the 'fox condo.'"

A low chuckle escaped him. Cassie felt it to her bones as she approached the fox. Her little goldish-red head lay propped on the grassy platform. "Look, Trace. That sweet face with all the white below. Have you ever seen anything like it? She's elegant. You would think she was gazing out at the whole world, seeing everything.

"Giselle?" The fox's ears pricked like Buttercup's. "Giselle? It's Cassie." The animal lifted her head and put her black nose to the fence. Cassie touched it with her finger. "I brought a friend. His name is Trace. Do you know what? He owns the ranch where you were found. Isn't that amazing?"

The fox moved its head as she talked.

"Good heavens. That animal understands you," Trace said under his breath. "I never saw anything like it."

"Then you haven't watched Liz talking to her horses. It's almost spooky the way they know everything she's saying. On her last round barrel racing at Finals, she had to ride Polly because Sunflower had gotten stall cast. She spoke to Polly the way I'm talking to you and told her they had to win for Connor. I swear that horse knew exactly what she had to do."

Their eyes met. "I wish I'd been there."

"You can't be everywhere while you're protecting our world from the air. But now that you're here, why don't you say something to Giselle? Let's see what she does. Touch her nose at the same time."

Trace moved closer and put his index finger on it. "Hello, Giselle. You don't know me. I'm Trace."

"Trace rhymes with Ace, Giselle. Guess what? Would you believe his eye got hurt, too? You two have a lot in common."

The man standing next to her threw back his head and laughed. It was a marvelous sound. Happy. Cassie wished he'd do it more often. When he quieted down he said, "Are you the one to name her Giselle?"

"Yes. The woman who ran this incredible French auberge in Switzerland had that name. I think it's beautiful, and it just seemed to suit my precious fox. I wanted to take her home with me to raise, but of course that was impossible. She was turned over to the sanctuary. That's when I started coming on a regular basis to help where I can.

"You should see all the animals and birds. They've got a rough-legged hawk that's only half-flighted, and a lynx that can only see light and dark. Then there's a vulture with an amputated wing. The list goes on and on."

Trace smiled at her. "Pretty soon you'll be occupied with your own little daughter. Maybe if the fox lives for a long time, you can bring her to see Giselle and tell her the story of how her daddy found the fox."

The tenderness in Trace's voice was too much. She felt her eyes smarting and fought tears. "Maybe."

"I'm sure you're tired. I'll follow you home. You've worked so hard, you need to put your feet up."

"You're not supposed to remember everything I tell you." Trace was way too attentive.

"My former commanding officer would tell me the exact opposite." He walked to her truck. "Drive safely." His eyes narrowed on her face. "Remember there are two of you to consider."

"As if I could forget," she said, sounding out of breath to her own ears. The things Trace said shook her world.

He got in his truck just as Paul called to her from outside his car. "See you next Saturday."

Cassie wheeled around. Lindsey smiled, giving Cassie a knowing look that said she approved of the attractive cowboy who'd come to the sanctuary looking for her. This town was too small for Trace and Cassie. Gossip would build. There'd be a price to pay if he didn't leave for Colorado soon.

"I'll be here, you guys. What will we be working on next?"

"That's anyone's guess. Let's go for pizza after."

"I'd love it."

Adrenaline spilled into her system as she drove back to the ranch. Out of her rearview mirror she noticed how Trace stayed behind her. She'd been alone just long enough without Logan that she'd forgotten what it was like to have someone watching out for her.

Cassie had to admit it was a nice feeling. She couldn't understand why Trace's girlfriend hadn't arrived here already. A man like him didn't come along every day. The Rafferty men were exceptional.

When she finally reached the ranch house, Trace pulled up alongside her and opened his window to talk to her. "Jarod called me a minute ago and asked me to meet up with him. Before I go, I want to make sure you get in the house safely."

Her spirits didn't know whether to be relieved or disappointed he was leaving. "I'm fine, Trace. Don't forget I've been doing this for a long time. But thanks for caring." She climbed down from the cab and hurried up the porch to the front door.

"Wait, Cassie—before you go in let's exchange cell

phone numbers in case we need to get hold of each other."

"That's a good idea." She pulled the phone out of her purse and programmed his number. He did the same thing with his phone. After opening the front door, she waved him off.

Who knew when he'd be back? *Please don't care, Cassie. Please don't.*

Once she showered, she'd grab a bite to eat and watch a little TV before going to bed. Maybe because she knew he would be coming back, even if it was late, Cassie was able to fall asleep faster. For the first time since Logan's passing, her husband didn't fill her thoughts. She found herself thinking about Trace and what an amazing man he was. Any woman loved by him would feel cherished.

TRACE DROVE OVER to Jarod's to pick him up. Jarod had talked to Zane after he and Avery had returned from the reservation. She was eager to visit her grandfather and tell him about her day, so Jarod thought this was the best time to drop in on Zane.

They took off for the Corkin-Lawson Ranch bordering the other side of the Bannock spread. "What does Avery do at the reservation?"

"She's a historian, writing a book on Crow folklore. On Thursdays she teaches classes on Crow culture at the college."

"You must be very proud of your sister."

"I am. The tribe has given her a special name. Winterfire Woman."

"What does it mean?"

"Because she does her research on the reservation year-round, not just in summer, the tribe considers her an authentic teller of their histories. She reminds them of the storytellers of old who gathered children around the fire on long wintry nights. Avery doesn't make them feel used."

"That's a phenomenal compliment. Are she and Zane happy?"

A smile broke the corner of Jarod's mouth. "You ought to see them together. I know she'll be anxious to see you."

It didn't take long for them to pull up in front of the small, one-story ranch house. They got out and knocked on the front door. Only one other time had Trace ever been over here. His father had been called out on an emergency and fifteen-year-old Trace had gone with him.

The owner of the ranch, Daniel Corkin, was in a drunken rage because his best horse had broken a leg. When his dad told him they needed to put the animal out of its misery, Daniel ordered him off his property. If he didn't leave, he'd shoot him.

Trace still remembered that day and understood why Daniel's daughter Sadie had fled to California to live with her mother, who later on remarried. His thoughts drifted back to Cassie. Her father Grant Bannock may not have been in a drunken rage, but he was unstable enough to drive his flesh-and-blood daughter out of his home and his life. Considering Ned Bannock was his son, it proved the adage that the proverbial acorn didn't fall far from the oak tree.

Trace's thoughts were jerked away when a striking man, Trace's height, in cowboy boots with dark brown hair answered the door. He wore a plaid shirt and jeans. "Thanks for coming, Jarod."

He nodded. "Zane Lawson? Meet Trace, Doc Rafferty's son."

His gray eyes swerved to examine Trace. Dimples formed when he smiled. "Your fame is legendary. Avery will be sorry she wasn't here to welcome you home, Trace. She's thrilled to know you're back to stay for good."

That meant Jarod hadn't told him about Trace's plans. Everyone assumed he was home to take over the ranch. "It'll be great to see her again."

"I'm finally shaking hands with the Ace!"

Trace liked him right away. "I'm a has-been. You're the famous SEAL."

"You couldn't be talking about me. My nephew Ryan has reduced me to Deputy Dawg status, isn't that right, Jarod."

All three men chuckled before Zane grew serious. "I know you have other things you'd rather do tonight, but I felt this visit couldn't wait, not after talking to Jarod. Come on in. Can I get you a drink?"

"No, thanks." They walked into the living room and sat down on the couch and chairs placed around the coffee table.

Zane eyed Trace. "Jarod said you've got something

to tell me pertaining to Ned I need to hear. He said it would be better coming from you. What's going on?"

For the next ten minutes Trace told him virtually what he'd told Jarod about his conversation with Owen Pearson, plus his own plans to sell the ranch. "Whoever the buyer is, I want all of you to approve. That includes Connor."

He saw Zane eye Jarod. "I can see why you felt this was important." Then his gaze switched to Trace. "I'm glad you haven't spoken to a Realtor yet. For your ranch to be put on the multiple listings, it could rip off the Band-Aid of a very old wound that has never healed."

"What do you mean?"

"How much do you know about the history between the Bannocks and the Corkins?"

"My dad told me Daniel Corkin has always had it in for the Bannocks. Something about oil, but he never knew the details."

"Then let me fill you in. Silas Bannock, a Scottish Presbyterian, drilled for oil on his property in 1915. At the time it was part of the Elk Basin Oil Field, and he hit a spewing gusher. Since it was on private land, he claimed all the money and built up the Bannock ranch. With wise investing over the years, Ralph Bannock has turned it into one of the wealthiest cattle ranches in Montana originally funded by oil."

Trace had no idea.

"In 1920, Pete Corkin, an English Methodist and neighbor of Silas Bannock, established the Corkin Ranch, the one we're sitting on right now. He drilled on this land and made some strikes that fizzled. In that same year Congress established a law that you had to lease federal land from the government and pay a royalty. Over the years, the Corkin descendants couldn't get rich by drilling for oil so they turned to cattle, and thus began a jealousy and a rivalry that developed into hostility."

Jarod sat forward and picked up the story. "Over the years this envy on the part of the Corkin family over our family's success escalated. Daniel Corkin swore he heard a story from one of his hands that a Crow Indian saw a vision about oil being under Corkin land.

"Convinced he'd be wealthier than the Bannocks when he made his strike, he became so obsessive about more drilling, his wife, Eileen, Sadie's mother, divorced him and went to her family in California. But he threatened to kill Eileen if she tried to take Sadie with her."

Trace couldn't believe what he'd just heard. "So that's why Sadie spent so much time with Liz's family."

Jarod nodded. "Daniel left the raising of Sadie to the Hensons, his foreman and wife. When Daniel died, he left nothing to Sadie in his will, and he made it impossible for any Bannock to buy the ranch. But that didn't hold up in a court of law. When the ranch was put on the market, Ned Bannock wanted it and was determined to buy it."

"Ned?"

"That's right. He was still in love with Sadie and wanted her, too. Using his father's and grandfather's money, he put in his bid with the Realtor. But my grandfather went to his attorney and we found a way to outbid him so Sadie could keep her property."

"They did it by helping me so I could buy it in my name," Zane interjected. "By that time I'd come from California with Sadie to help her raise Ryan, who is my brother Tim's son. I wanted to start a new life here after both Tim and my wife died. This property is now called the Corkin-Lawson Ranch. It'll be my nephew Ryan's legacy one day." His voice grew husky. "I'll be indebted to Jarod and his grandfather forever for what they did for Sadie and for me."

"But we still have a big problem," Jarod interjected. "Like Daniel, Ned is still convinced there's oil under all our ranches. On his last birthday three weeks ago, he came into his inheritance. The second he hears that you've put the Rafferty ranch on the market, he'll forget his idea to go in on a feral stud farm with Owen, and use the money to buy your ranch. In his sick mind, he'll want it so he can drill for oil and be wealthier than anyone. Then Sadie will want him."

"That's really sick, Jarod."

"You don't know the half of it."

"Jarod's right," Zane said. "In my mind Ned is a sociopath. Maybe he didn't kill Logan. That I have yet to discover. But he tried to kill Jarod."

"I know. Last night Cassie told me about the therapy sessions. They revealed that Ned has always hated her."

"He's been jealous of his sister and brothers, my cousins, and me for as long as I've known him," Jarod murmured.

Trace eyed both men. "I can tell she's afraid."

Zane grimaced. "With good reason."

Jarod said, "The other day Grandfather told me and

Connor that according to Uncle Grant, Ned has been a model patient and his doctors feel he's ready to come home for good. But none of us believes it. There's something wrong in Ned's nature. If he gets upset, he'll go after anyone who gets in his way."

"After what happened to Logan, Cassie has to be terrified," Trace said.

"That's why Uncle Grant has always been afraid of Ned. We have a situation we're going to have to handle." Jarod got to his feet. "Sorry to have held you up, Zane, but I felt this was important for you to hear."

"It's vital," Zane replied. "If you're intent on selling the ranch, Trace, get it done discreetly by private sale. Hopefully Ned won't find out about it until long after it's a fait accompli. As for Cassie, she knows she'll always have a home with us."

"Or me or Connor," Jarod exclaimed. "Now that she's pregnant, she's going to need family. We're all going to have to help keep her safe."

Trace got to his feet. "You two have given me a lot to think about."

Zane walked them outside. "Let's keep in close touch from here on out. Now that you're retired from the Air Force, I know Avery wants to give a party to welcome you home."

"That sounds terrific."

"Words can't tell you how sorry we are about your eye injury."

"It's nothing compared to the many guys who've lost lives."

Trace waved Zane off before they drove away and

headed for Jarod's house. The conversation had increased his fears for Cassie's welfare. Jarod slanted him a piercing glance.

"With you back, it feels like the circle is complete once more."

Emotion thickened his throat. "It's great being with you again, Jarod. I'd forgotten just how much I've missed my oldest friends."

"Then prove it and stay put." He got out of the truck. "We'll talk again soon."

"Yup. Tell Sadie hi for me."

Trace drove back to the ranch, hoping Cassie was still up. There was a lot he needed to say to her. But when he walked inside, it was quiet and he knew she'd gone to bed. After talking with Jarod and Zane, he could see things were more complicated than he would have imagined. Nothing was black-and-white.

When he got ready for bed, he remembered what his doctor had said about working things out with Nicci before he made any decisions. Trace fell asleep frustrated that she hadn't called him today. His last thoughts were of Jarod telling him to stay put.

LATE SUNDAY MORNING he came awake to the smell of strawberries drifting through the house. Cassie was at it again. He was glad she hadn't gone anywhere yet. He was glad her brother wasn't back living on the Bannock Ranch yet.

Content that she and the baby were safe for the moment, Trace could relax while he thought about the conversation with his father yesterday. "Before you make a decision you can't take back, why not rent the house for the next year, son, to give yourself time?"

In the light of morning his father's suggestion made sense. The right renter would pay a lot for the use of the house sitting on prime hunting land. If Trace charged enough money, his father would receive substantial monthly payments that would add appreciably to his income.

Once he was working in Colorado Springs, Trace could fly to Billings for a weekend once a month to see his father and inspect the property. It could work. How would Nicci feel about it? He needed her to come! The doctor in Billings was right. There was no way he could make definite plans about anything until they were together and could make a decision about getting married.

He rolled onto his side and reached for the phone to call her. To his chagrin it went through to her voice mail. Trace asked her to get in touch with him as soon as she could. Had she refused to answer his calls on purpose? They needed to talk before any more time went by.

Once he'd showered and dressed, he walked through the house and heard voices in the kitchen. One of them was male. Connor! A smile broke out on his face as he entered. "Well if it isn't the king of the rodeo!"

"Dude!" His dark blond friend made a beeline for him and gave him one of those hugs he was famous for—one that could throw a bull to the ground in a couple of seconds. No one had ever called him that but Connor.

"I thought you were injured at finals, but I swear you're tougher than ever."

Connor let out a bark of laughter. "Don't I wish, but you're looking ripped. How in the hell did you run into a laser?"

Cassie stood in the background, dressed in a blue-and-green print top and jeans. The pregnant woman was beautiful no matter what she wore. Her gaze swerved from Trace to her cousin. "It ran into *him*, Connor. Kind of the way that steer bucked upward and tore your shoulder. Talk about the walking wounded around here, but no one would ever know looking at the two of you!"

Both men chuckled. Connor's blue eyes twinkled as he studied her. "I guess you thought you could keep *your* condition a secret, sweetie pie. But Jarod and I had our suspicions a month ago when we saw you leading Masala around instead of riding him. Liz and Sadie are already fighting over who's going to get to babysit your daughter."

Trace eyed Connor. "Did she show you the ultrasound picture yet? It's like a miracle."

"No." Connor shot him a speculative glance. "I haven't had that privilege. Cassie? Can I see it, too? Liz and I are trying for a baby."

"I know."

"What do you mean you know?"

"At your wedding reception Liz whispered to me that giving you a child would be her top priority in the foreseeable future."

"Apparently there are no secrets."

"Nope—I'll run to the bedroom and get it."

In another minute she was back. Trace smiled at her before he took the picture from her and showed it to Connor. While they tried to pick out all the parts, Cassie finished a batch of jam.

Connor let out a whistle. "Your baby's going to be a real knockout."

"You're full of it, cousin."

"That wasn't nice. I may not have been born with Jarod's gift of vision, but I can say without any doubt that your baby's going to be just like her mother. You brought every cowboy in Carbon County to your doorstep in high school."

"Stop, Connor. You're embarrassing me in front of Trace."

"Why? You know it's true and Trace is practically family. You broke so many hearts when you went away to Missoula, it took me and Jarod at least a year to pick up the pieces you left behind. I think Russ Colby still hasn't married because of you."

"That's absurd."

"Nope. He stopped me at the supermarket the other day, wanting to know how you were getting along since the funeral. I could swear he was nervous and it wouldn't surprise me if you hear from him one of these days. I know what you're going to say. That it's too soon since Logan's passing, but I just thought you ought to know."

Trace wouldn't be surprised either. When he'd taken Cassie to that film on Friday night, every male in creation was aware of her. It wasn't just her exceptional looks a man found appealing. She glowed.

When he'd first seen her in the garden at the side of the house, he was drawn to her in a way he hadn't been to another woman besides Nicci. But he could tell Connor's comments were getting to her.

He put the picture on the table. "Have you got time to ride with me this morning?"

"That's why I'm here." Trace could read between the lines. Connor had already been in communication with his brother and Zane.

"Good. Then we'll get out of your hair for a while, Cassie."

She darted Trace what could be a grateful smile. "When you get back I'll have lunch waiting for you."

"I'm looking forward to it already," Connor said over his shoulder. They left through the back door and headed for the barn. The sky had become overcast. "It might rain later."

"Maybe."

"Jarod told me you handled Masala like he was your horse. You ride him while I take Buttercup."

In a few minutes the horses were bridled, but both men rode bareback. They headed for the forest and rode as far as the second stream crossing the property. "When I think of the years we used to ride all over the Pryors…" Connor murmured. "It's great to have you back, Trace."

"I'm afrai—"

"Save it," Connor cut him off. "I know all about your plans to get out of Dodge, but you can't do it."

"I'm planning to get married."

"I know all about that, too. You don't honestly think you'll be happy at the Air Force Academy. It won't work. I'll give you a month at best before you want out. Anything less than flying again and you'll hate it. You're a crack pilot, Trace, but those days are over."

"But if I stay here and work the ranch, I've a feeling in my gut Nicci won't like it."

"How soon is she coming?"

"I don't know. I'm waiting to hear any day now."

"Well don't do anything about the ranch until you've spent time with her here. It would be a waste to take her to Colorado Springs. You're a cowboy to the roots, Trace. What would you have done if there'd been no injury? What if you'd finished out all those years as a pilot? Then what? Stay in Italy for the rest of your life away from your father? Doing what?"

Trace took a swift breath. "I've been asking myself that question since I was released from the hospital. I know what Nicci would want. She'd expect me to go on living there while her father found work for me."

"No way," Connor muttered. "When I married Reva, I thought I had it all figured out until she came home with me for a time. Our marriage took a nosedive. We could never get it back because it never worked in the first place. The ranch was my life. Hers was in the city."

"I know. Cassie told me. Reva and my mother had a lot in common."

"That's right, but with one difference. We weren't pregnant so it was easier to say goodbye. So learn from my mistake and take a leaf out of my book while you're still free. Forget Colorado. You don't really want to teach other guys how to fly. You've been there and done that.

"Bring Nicci to the ranch and let her get a taste of

what life will be like with you. This is your home. Ask her to stay here and find out if she takes to it. Otherwise I can promise you'll be miserable, and that's without the benefit of Jarod's special gift telling you the same thing. We don't want anyone else living next door."

"You and Jarod know how to make a guy feel good. I'll think about everything you've said. But there's still the problem of Cassie to worry about."

"It's been solved. Liz has already talked to her mom. Millie and Mac are going to keep Cassie with them until after the baby is born. She'll be close by all of us and safe with them."

"That's a terrific solution, but Cassie won't do it. She's too independent."

"She will when Zane talks to her. Jarod found out from our grandfather that Ned is being released from the mental facility a week from Thursday." *Eleven more days*... "Because of the suspicion surrounding the reason for Logan's shooting, he wants her away from your ranch. Mac Henson will be the best body-guard she could have."

Trace pondered everything. "When were you going to talk to Cassie?"

"After lunch I was hoping to take her over to our house where Liz and I will broach the subject."

"Do me a favor and let me discuss that with her, Connor?" Several ideas were rolling around in his head now that he'd heard the date of Ned's release from the facility. A new, possible option had opened up in his mind, but he wasn't prepared to address it yet. "I need to tell Cassie about my plans for the ranch before she hears it from anyone else. Dad and I owe her that much after the fabulous way she and Logan have taken care of everything."

After a moment of quiet, "Sure, Trace. We just want you to know we're here for her in any capacity. And you."

"Thanks, Connor."

"That's what best friends are for, right?"

"You know it."

They headed back to the barn to give the horses water and fresh hay. When they entered the kitchen, Cassie had made them tuna fish and peanut butter sandwiches. She'd also put two quarts of milk on the table, unopened, and a bowl of potato chips. Trace couldn't help but smile at her. "Trust you to know exactly what to fix."

"It's easy when you're feeding a bunch of ravenous cowboys," she quipped.

Did she really see Trace that way?

After they'd eaten, Connor thanked Cassie and excused himself to get back to Liz. Trace walked him out to the porch and waved him off. When he returned to the kitchen, the clock on the wall said it was ten after two.

Cassie had cleaned everything up and was packing her jam jars in some cartons.

"Need me to help?"

"Oh, no. I'm all done. Thanks, though."

She wouldn't look at him. "Who's the lucky recipient?"

"Hopefully my baby. I plan to sell these at the White

Lodge Fair in the fall so I can buy some essentials. You know. A crib and an infant car seat. Things like that. My time will be here before I know it. I need to be prepared."

"Cassie?"

"Yes?"

"If you don't have plans, how would you like to take a Sunday ride with me? Not a long one. I haven't been up to Yellow Bell Lake in years. There won't be many people around in case you're worried about that." He figured they'd beat the rain if it came.

She turned her head to look at him. "I'm sure you have other things you need to be doing."

He stared at her through veiled eyes. "Talking to you is at the top of my list."

Chapter Five

That sounded somewhat ominous because there was no
levity now that Connor had gone. Trace would never
invite Cassie to go out with him unless he had a heavy
reason.

"You want to leave right away?"

"If it's all right with you."

"Of course. I'll just grab my purse."

In a few minutes they'd both freshened up. He
brought a bottle of water for each of them. After helping her into his Explorer, he walked around to his side
and they took off. After they pulled out on the highway,
he turned at the next left leading up the mountain to a
number of lakes hidden in the pines.

The small circular lake was named for the yellow
bells that blossomed there in the spring. But when Trace
pulled into the area where he could park the car, he
could see that time was over for this year.

"I'm afraid it's too late for the flowers to be in
bloom," she said, reading his mind.

"It's still a beautiful spot, even with the cloud cover.
Your cousins and I used to ride our horses up here when

the ground was covered in a mass of tiny yellow bells. We'd swim and have rock-skipping contests."

She nodded. "I rode up here with my high school friends, too. Marsha Porter's dad would drive up with the inner tubes so we could float and sunbathe. I'm sure the music scared away every wild creature in sight. Those were fun, lazy days until—"

When she didn't finish the sentence Trace glanced at her. "Until Ned ruined things?"

"I don't want to talk about him."

"I think we're going to have to at some point. What do you say we get out and sit on that log the guys and I dragged over there once upon a time."

Her eyes widened. "You did that?"

"It was either that or sit in the wet grass."

Cassie chuckled and got out before he could come around to help her. "It's lovely up here. I'd almost forgotten." She made her way over to the log. "Oh, my gosh—your initials! TR, CB and JB." Cassie lifted her head. "Okay. Truth time. How many girls did you bring up here?"

His lips twitched. "We swore an oath we'd never tell."

"Well, we all know who Jarod brought, so that's no mystery. Connor probably had dozens up here at one time or other. Besides Liz, Marsha had a terrible crush on him. Then there's *you*. Since you went to high school in Billings, you were the mystery man of the three amigos. Did you have a special girlfriend?"

"I dated, but didn't bring anyone up here." His eyes

zeroed in on her. "You're the first. To prove it, I'll carve your initials next to mine."

"No, Trace. Stop!"

But he'd pulled out a Swiss army knife and carved so fast she couldn't believe it.

"There—CBD."

Her heart pounded like a runaway train.

"I think you're trying to sweeten me up before you drop a bomb on me."

He put the knife back in his jeans pocket and straddled the log near where she was sitting.

His right boot almost touched hers. Being with him like this away from the world caused her to think forbidden thoughts. She despised her vulnerability and—heaven help her—her susceptibility to everything male in him.

Cassie sneaked a glance at his handsome features made more severe by whatever serious thoughts were going on inside him.

"You need to know something important. I can't put this off any longer. It wouldn't be fair to you. My father gave me the ranch as my legacy, but my intention is to sell it."

She averted her eyes, too shocked by his announcement to make a sound. Poor, dear Sam.

"By the crestfallen look on your face, I can tell this has come as a blow. If I tell you the reason why, I know it won't take away the shock, but I hope you'll understand this is something I have to do. Dad and Ellen need the money to buy themselves a house."

"You don't owe me an explanation, Trace. It doesn't

have anything to do with me. Logan and I were lucky to find work here for as long as we could."

"Cassie—" he said in an urgent voice. "Please realize it won't happen right away. I want you to stay on and earn your living until I find a buyer. Or maybe a renter. Probably within four to six weeks. Hopefully that will give you enough time to make other arrangements. I'm prepared to help you with that. So is your family."

"What do you mean?"

"Connor told me that Mac and Millie want you to live with them until after your baby is born where you'll be safe. That's the reason he came over earlier, but I told him I'd rather tell you myself."

"I see." She got to her feet and walked over to the water's edge. "That's all very kind of the family, but I'll make my own arrangements."

She felt him behind her. "I told Connor that's what you'd say because you're much too independent."

"You know me well. Do you mind if we go home now? It's going to rain." They'd heard thunder, so it wouldn't be long.

His hands slid to her shoulders. He pulled her back against his hard-muscled body. The unexpected action caused a small gasp to escape her lips. "I meant what I said about helping you. The Realtor I'm using can find you a place to live at the same time."

"I'm sure he could, but I'll be fine." Before she turned around and crumbled in his arms, Cassie eased away from him and walked back to the car. By the time he'd joined her, she'd put one of the bottles of water to her lips.

"Cassie—"

"I want to thank you for being frank with me so I can handle this on my own. Four to six weeks gives me enough time to find work and a place to live that suits me. I knew this day had to come. It's another wake-up call after being in a deep sleep. You and your father have been so kind and wonderful to me, I'll never be able to thank you enough."

Fat drops of water started to hit the windshield as they started down the mountain. Slow at first, they picked up speed until there was a downpour. By the time she and a tight-lipped Trace reached the ranch, she felt as if they'd been enclosed in their own secret world. She was unbearably aware of him. Something about the rain made everything more intimate. His chiseled profile haunted her.

When he stopped the car, she jumped out, needing to get away from him. Once in the house she rushed to her bedroom and shut the door. Hoping to shrug off the feel of his hands on her shoulders, Cassie got undressed and took a shower.

She washed her hair and pampered herself, but the imprint of his body against her back still stayed with her. When desire hit, there was no mistaking it for anything else. She desired Trace Rafferty. How long had he been at the ranch? Six days? Up at the lake he'd carved her initials in the log and she'd responded like a love-struck teenager instead of a twenty-seven-year-old pregnant woman.

When she finally left her room in a clean pair of denims and a cotton sweater, the house was quiet. After looking out the living room window she discovered his Explorer was still there, but he wasn't inside the house. With the storm activity, he was probably out at the barn to settle the horses. Thank heaven. She needed some breathing space.

While he was gone, she fixed them each a sandwich and left a covered plate on the table for him. She took her sandwich back to her room. How long ago had Trace dropped his bomb on Sam? Had it happened while the two men had sat out on the front porch swing that first night?

She was still trying to recover from the direct hit she'd taken after learning about his plans. Doc Rafferty would be sick over his son's decision to live in Colorado, but as she'd told Trace, it was none of her business.

Cassie should be thankful he'd been up-front with her this afternoon. Trace had given her enough time to find a new job she badly needed. Her college degree in wildlife conservation from the University of Montana in Missoula could open doors for her. She would hunt for jobs with the government, but her first choice would be to work in the private sector.

The White Lodge Wildlife Sanctuary might be a good place to start looking since she already had a connection there. It depended on one of their paid staff leaving, but she didn't know what the odds were of that happening. If she found a decent apartment to rent in town, the location would be perfect.

She could approach the owners at the sanctuary and find out if they were planning to hire someone else. With her college credentials and her work with the American Prairie Reserve after she'd graduated, it was possible they might hire her. The two years she'd spent on the High Plains in northeastern Montana helping facilitate and maintain water rights along with livestock and wildlife had given her invaluable training.

It was on one of her brief trips home she'd met Logan Dorney, the new hired hand on the Bannock Ranch. Technically speaking, Jarod had done the hiring. When Cassie's father had fired him, Jarod didn't override the decision. Sadie confided to Cassie that her husband felt it was wise to leave it alone. Everyone, especially Jarod, knew how fragile Cassie's father had become because of Ned.

If Cassie and Logan hadn't fallen in love, she'd still be working in the northeast part of the state. With that on her resume, it was worth it to find out if the sanctuary would be interested in her.

Tomorrow after breakfast she'd drive into town and make a start. If there was no opening, she'd run by the fish-and-game office to see what they'd posted locally. After that she'd drop in at the Bureau of Indian Affairs.

A water conservancy group was doing a project out on the Pryor Crow Reservation an hour away from White Lodge. Maybe she could get hired on there, but they preferred to employ an Apsáalooke. She understood that. Still, if they needed someone qualified and no one else had applied, she could get lucky and be hired.

Cassie was desperate for a good job and wouldn't stop until she found one.

For the next hour she looked up all kinds of positions in her field on her laptop. Helena and Kalispell had half a dozen wildlife conservancy openings, but she didn't want to move to either place away from Avery and her cousins' wives. Sadie and Liz had been her friends from grade school. With Logan gone, she needed them, even if they didn't get together very often.

Though Trace had said she could stay here until the new owner moved in, she knew she was living on borrowed time. Tomorrow she'd go to town and start looking for an apartment. The small nest egg she'd saved from the insurance money would make it possible for her to put down a cleaning deposit, plus first and last month's rent.

As soon as she could move in, hopefully next week with Avery's help, she'd drop by the vet clinic and turn in the house key to Sam. If her applications for work didn't produce results soon, then she'd get a temporary job in town until the right one came along. Having made up her mind, she could finally settle down to sleep.

But when she got ready for bed and crawled under the covers, she soon broke down in agony and reached for the picture of her husband she kept on the bedside table. "Logan...why did you have to die? I need you more than ever now. I don't know how I'm going to make it." Tears soaked her pillow as she fell, finally, into a fitfull sleep.

TRACE CHECKED ON the horses to make sure the storm hadn't bothered them. There'd been some lightning and thunder. Content they were all right, he went back in the house and found a couple of sandwiches waiting for him.

She was amazing. He decided there wasn't anything she couldn't do in spite of her pain.

After he'd finished eating, he started down the hall to his room when he heard anguished sobs coming from the other side of Cassie's door. It tore his guts out. He felt guilty as hell.

Not only had he devastated his father with his unwelcome news on that first night, Trace was now forcing Cassie to find a new job while she was still grief-stricken over the loss of her husband. But no one could bring Logan Dorney back.

No one could give Trace a new eye so he could continue to fly.

No one could make his father ten years younger so he and Ellen could enjoy the ranch together.

No magic formula could take away Nicoletta's pain because the work he needed to do was here in the United States. Their dream to live in Italy had been shattered by that laser.

No wrinkle in time could put Trace's family back together before the divorce.

Some things weren't fixable.

Full of grief himself, he left the house and walked around to the garden, thankful his father had Ellen to cling to at this time in his life.

The rain had stopped and the storm clouds had moved on. In the distance loomed the shadow of the Pryor Mountains. They were sacred to the Crow Nation whose people called them the Hitting Rocks Mountains because of the abundance of flint.

The Pryors weren't as high or as spectacular as the Italian Dolomites where he'd done a lot of mountain climbing and skiing, but they had their own unique beauty. Over the years he and his father had ridden into them hundreds of times. They would wind around the canyons where wild horses like Masala roamed free. The sight of them thundering through a gully took your breath.

Trace walked down one of the rows of fruit and reached for some strawberries that had ripened. The rain hadn't hurt them. They were delicious. Cassie's jam was to die for. So were her rolls and the roast and meatloaf she'd cooked last week, the kind he'd eaten as a boy. He hadn't had much of an appetite since his injury. But the food he'd enjoyed since coming to the ranch had conjured memories of home long ago when his life had been intact, and he'd found he couldn't get enough of it.

Food could do that to you—send you to a place in your mind. Trace had been around the world. Every country had its own specialties. But only one place served food that reminded him of his childhood. Today at the lake, tonight in the barn tending to the horses, he was shaken by emotions he hadn't allowed to surface for a long time. They would smother him if he didn't do something concrete about his situation.

First thing in the morning he would contact Bud Hawksworth, the Realtor in Billings, and ask him to keep his sights out for someone who wanted to buy a ranch like Rafferty's. No putting it on the multiple listings. With the fall hunting season coming up, this time of year would be the best time to make the most of a profitable sale.

Cassie had turned him down flat when he'd suggested

the Realtor would be able to help her find a place. It could kill two birds with one stone, but she wasn't having any of it. He shouldn't have said it. Cassie was fiercely in charge of her own life. His respect for her continued to grow. *So did his attraction.* That alarmed him.

When he'd pulled her against him at the lake, it had taken every bit of willpower not to turn her around and kiss her whether he had her permission or not. To do that would end any trust and she'd be out the door and gone in a shot.

He needed to put the desire to make love to her behind him. They'd start fresh at breakfast. But when he got up the next morning and eventually went to the kitchen after a shower and shave, he discovered a note she'd left on the counter.

Trace,

I didn't want to wake you, so I left your breakfast in the oven. If you feel like strawberries, they're in a bowl in the fridge. There's some ham and rolls for lunch if you get hungry before my return. I made a fresh pot of coffee before I walked out the door. I'll be back by afternoon to do your wash and anything else you might want done. You already have my cell phone in case you need to get in touch with me.

C.

He shook his head. Trace had never had service like

this in his life. She took the role of housekeeper to a new level.

When he opened the oven door he discovered bacon and scrambled eggs just the way he liked them. Her husband had been a lucky man. After pouring himself a cup of coffee, he took everything to the table and phoned the Realty company while he ate. The secretary said Bud would return the call once he was free.

WHEN CASSIE HAD gotten up early on Monday, she'd been relieved to discover Trace's Explorer was still out in front, which meant he was in bed. After making breakfast for both of them, she got on the computer to see what rentals were listed. Instead of printing out the ones she wanted, she could pull them up on her smart-phone and leave for White Lodge now. She was determined to find a place to live ASAP so she could start planning a nursery.

By midafternoon she'd found an eight-plex apartment house near the center of town with floor plans she liked, but the ground-floor apartment she wanted wouldn't be vacant until two weeks from now. But before she paid money, she needed to see it empty. The landlord agreed to hold it for her if she left a refundable deposit in case she didn't want it. They made an appointment for her to come back then. If all went well she'd sign a year lease.

Tomorrow being Tuesday, she'd spend part of the day putting up more jam. When she'd finished she would drive over to Connor's ranch house. Since she was moving, she couldn't keep her horses. If he didn't know someone who would like to buy them, he would know how she should advertise to get the best results.

Trace was home when she returned. She found him in the living room eating potato chips while he watched a rerun of an NFL football game on TV. The second he saw her, he turned it off and got to his feet. He looked amazing in a black crewneck shirt and jeans. "You've been gone a long time."

She bit her lip. "I had a lot to do. How was your day?"

"Good. I spent most of it with my Dad."

"How is he?"

"Fine."

"I'm glad." She turned to leave.

"The horses are happy."

"That's good."

"How are you?"

"Tired. I'm going to bed. Have a nice evening."

"Cassie? Wait—" he said as she started for the hallway.

Her heart pounded. She glanced at him. "What is it?"

"Have I offended you in some way?"

"Of course not!"

His hands went to his hips in a male stance. "Something's bothering you. Can we talk about it in more than monosyllabic words?"

That was her fault. She was being rude. "Sorry if I came across uncommunicative. Let's agree we both have a lot on our minds."

"Do you want to talk?"

She shook her head. "No."

"Well *I* do. Today I happened to see your truck in

front of an apartment complex with a for-rent sign in the manager's apartment window. Has my presence made you so uncomfortable, you're considering moving out right now?"

Oh, boy. She should have known. White Lodge was such a small town, you couldn't get away with much.

Cassie lifted her head and stared straight at him. "After Mandy saw me out with you the night we went to the film, I realized how it must have looked to her. Your dad is a prominent man in town and people are finding out you're back home. Friends like the people I volunteer with know I'm still living here on your ranch. But all it takes is one troublemaker to spread rumors about you and me living under the same roof together. They don't know you're moving to Colorado."

She watched him rub the back of his neck. It meant he was listening.

"You know what I mean, Trace—the grieving widow and the hotshot bachelor pilot. Soon it will be all over town that I'm pregnant. I can just imagine the spin some people will put on it, saying that the last time you came to visit your father, you must have hooked up with the housekeeper when her husband wasn't around."

"No one would think that!"

"Yes they would and you know it."

His silence said it all.

"There's a base element of society that exists everywhere, Trace. We can solve the problem by not being seen together. The damage may already have been done when Ned hears about it from his friends. They visit him and have regular contact. Once he finds out you're back and were seen with his pregnant sister, it could start a wildfire of gossip. I've told you he hates me. You'd be surprised just how ugly it could get."

Trace stood. "I know you're frightened of him, but since he's still living in the mental health facility, you don't need to be in a rush. I had a long talk about him with Zane and Jarod. When and if Ned is released, you have a home with your cousins who plan to protect you."

Her face went hot, something it had been doing a lot since Trace had shown up in the fruit garden. "I know my cousins would do anything for me, but I would never impose on their lives that way because of Ned. They're all newlyweds for heaven's sake!"

"But you're forgetting one thing. If Ned is released soon, they're not going to let you live in town by yourself."

"Then I'll move to another part of the state!" she fired back.

Trace shifted his weight. "We're getting ahead of ourselves. For now I'm here to keep an eye on you until I leave for Colorado Springs. Until then, this is your home."

"It's *not* my home!" Cassie exclaimed. "Your father left the ranch to you. Hopefully I'll be able to move to the apartment in two weeks when it will be vacant."

"Have you put money down yet?"

"A deposit. I want to see it without any furnishings. If I like it, then I'll sign a year's lease."

"Where are *your* furnishings? None of your things are here."

"They're in storage," she lied.

Trace's eyes looked pained. "I can't let you leave because of what a few people might say, Cassie."

"Please stop feeling guilty. I can handle anything but that."

"If I'd known what was going to happen, I would never have suggested we drive into town to see a film."

"Please don't say that. Don't you know I'm glad Mandy saw us together? It got me going sooner on finding my own place to live. I need to get ready for the baby. This is all for the best. In four or five weeks when this place is sold, I'll be another month along. I'd rather move now while I'm in good shape. That apartment is perfect for me."

His dark brows furrowed. "But you don't have a job yet."

"I'll get one. I know almost every store owner in White Lodge. If I can't work in my chosen field for a while, I can always get a job at one of their businesses. Today I saw a dozen help-wanted signs in the shop windows."

"That kind of work isn't for you, especially not at this stage in your pregnancy."

"Don't be ridiculous. I'm perfectly healthy."

"And I want you to stay that way."

"I *am* over twenty-one and in charge of myself. You're sounding like a husband—" she blurted before she realized her mistake. Heat washed over her in waves. "I—I'm sorry," she stammered. "I didn't mean to say that."

The faint glimmer of a smile hovered on his lips. "I'm sorry I provoked you. Chalk it up to the picture of your sonogram. Since looking at it, your pregnancy is very real to me. I don't like being the person who is causing these sudden drastic changes in your life. I want to fix everything. Since learning more about Ned's instability, I intend to keep you safe."

Cassie knew he meant it, and it touched her heart. "That's not your job. When I move, everything's fixed. It's that simple. Tomorrow I'm going to ask Connor if he knows anyone who would like to buy the horses."

"When the time comes, I can help with that. While I have time on my hands waiting for a potential buyer, I'll move everything from your storage unit into your apartment."

"You mean you've decided I'm allowed to make my own decisions and move out of here?"

He shrugged his broad shoulders. "It appears there's no stopping you."

"Good. I'm glad we understand each other." She took a deep breath. "Just so we're clear, I won't need your help during the move."

He walked closer to her. "Naturally your cousins will be there for you, but I'm the one creating all the disturbance, so I intend to repair the damage."

"There's no damage, Trace, and I'd rather you didn't."

"Why?" he demanded in a quiet, yet compelling, tone. She knew he'd keep it up until he got the answer he wanted.

"Because there *are* no furnishings."

He frowned. "What do you mean?"

"I didn't want you to know. Logan and I moved into this house without any possessions of our own except our clothes and a few personal items. My father forbade me to take one thing from my home."

"I don't believe a parent could be that cruel."

She clenched her hands. "He thought that if I left destitute, I'd cave and decide not to marry Logan. Luckily my husband owned his own truck. We lived at a motel for a week before moving into your father's completely furnished house. All of the furniture and pictures must be heartbreakingly familiar to you."

Fists formed at his sides. "He literally threw you out?" Trace had ignored her comments about the house.

"Yes," she whispered, blinking hard to keep her eyes from tearing.

"Didn't your brothers want to help you?"

"Afraid not. We have a dysfunctional family with a capital *D*."

"So when you rent the apartment, you have nothing to put in it?"

"Nothing, except for personal possessions. But that's not a problem. I'm planning to make the rounds of the yard sales and find what I need."

"Then we'll do it together."

"What? And cause even more gossip?" Her questions bounced against the walls of the house. "I have friends to help me. It's not your concern. I'll buy a new bed and crib from the furniture store and have them delivered. It will all work out."

"The hell it will."

"Careful, Captain. You're not in the military now." The second the words left her mouth, Cassie wished she could call them back. "I'm sorry, Trace. That was another terrible, thoughtless thing to say to you. I keep doing it. Forgive me."

"It's my fault," he said in a quiet voice. "I've done a terrible thing by badgering you."

"Neither of us is at our best. I'm missing Logan who's never going to come back. You're missing Nicoletta, but you're fortunate because she'll be flying over soon."

"Cassie—"

"Don't interrupt me. Please," she begged. "Can't you see how much better it will be when I'm gone so she can stay here with you alone? The two of you will be able to make plans for your future."

"I'm afraid it won't be that simple."

"Give her some time to get acquainted with your world, Trace. Take her to Colorado Springs, then come back here. Who knows? Maybe she'll love it here more and want to be a rancher's wife. I guarantee that seeing you again, she'll want to marry you on the spot."

His head lifted. "That's because you grew up a Montana girl and love of the Pryors is burned deep inside you, but it's not for everyone. My mother never took to this life."

"I always wondered about her. How did your parents get together?"

"They met in Yellowstone Park while she was on vacation with some friends from Denver. Dad had just finished attending a veterinarian conference in Salt Lake and stopped there on his way back to Montana. He urged her to come and see him in White Lodge.

One thing led to another and they got married, but she missed living in a big city and complained a lot."

"That would have been incredibly painful for you."

"It was. When she asked for the divorce, Dad begged her not to move so far away he couldn't see me when he wanted. So she moved to Billings and eventually met a man from there. They married, and now he works for a company in Portland."

"Your father never met anyone else?"

"There were women, but his hurt went deep. It made me glad when he met Ellen and wanted to marry her."

"Your dad seems to be so happy."

"He was until I came home and hurt him all over again."

"Not deliberately, Trace."

"You're very sweet, Cassie." He lounged against the back of the couch. "How's the job hunting coming?"

"I've made applications at several places. Now it's a waiting game. All I can do is hope to be contacted for a first interview. You know how that goes. Except that *you* never went through that process. The Air Force wanted you immediately."

"Where did you get an idea like that?"

"Your father."

He shook his head. "What did you study at the university?"

When she told him about her college degree in wild-life conversation and experience with the American Prairie Reserve, he said, "I should think any of those places where you applied would be eager to hire you. With all those credentials, you blow me away."

"Thanks. I'm hoping someone will give me a call back."

"If Jarod knew about your application for the job on the reservation, he'd do whatever he could to help you."

"I know, but I need to do this on my own merits."

He smiled. "If I didn't know anything else about you, I know that."

"So is anyone interested in buying the ranch yet?"

Trace had hesitated talking about it, but since she brought it up, he might as well tell her the truth. "I heard back from my Realtor this afternoon. He's going to put out some feelers, but not on the multiple listing. I've decided to keep this as quiet as possible. Naturally I'll let you know when he's found someone who wants to come out to the ranch to look around."

"It's a choice piece of property and this house is darling." Her voice throbbed.

"That's because you and Logan made this place your own and it shows. I feel worse than ever over the new situation facing you."

"Please don't. With that eye injury you have your own cross to bear. For your sake, let's hope the ranch is taken off the market in no time."

"We'll see. Now I've kept you up too long. Get a good sleep."

"You, too. Good night."

Chapter Six

Tuesday morning Trace had just come in after a ride on Masala when his cell rang. Hoping it was Nicci phoning him, he jumped down from the horse and let him run in the paddock. But when he looked at the caller ID, it was the Realtor. He clicked On.

"Mr. Hawksworth?"

"Bud, please."

"All right. I didn't expect a call from you this soon."

"Are you kidding? A ranch like yours will be a piece of cake to sell. I've got some great news already."

Trace braced himself. "Go ahead."

"I keep a list of preferred clients who want to be notified if something they've been looking for suddenly comes on the market. One in particular is a potential buyer with money from the East Coast whose family is into the manufacturing business. His name is Lamont Walker. When I called him about your property, he said it was exactly what he was looking for and can meet your ballpark price. In a word, he was *ecstatic*."

The unexpected news twisted unpleasantly in Trace's

gut. This was all happening too fast. "Tell me about him."

"He's a big game hunter who would use the ranch for hunting parties with his friends throughout the year when he's not off to Africa."

Already Trace didn't like the sound of him. The man had no plan to do any ranching. No interest in raising crops or running cattle. He'd have to hire someone to look after the place when he was gone on safari.

"Mr. Walker has his own company jet and is already on his way to Billings after being in Chicago on business. He'll come to my office tomorrow before we drive to your ranch."

Tomorrow? "Does he have family?"

"He's forty-seven and divorced. That's all I know. I have to tell you that this is absolutely the right kind of buyer who knows what he wants and is ready to strike while the iron's hot. I'll let you know what time you can expect us at the ranch."

Trace wasn't ready for this, but it was too late to put him off now. Bud Hawksworth was a go-getter. Probably the best in the business.

"I'll look out for your call, Bud. Thank you."

CASSIE LOVED HER cousins and Liz. No one had a more loving extended family than she did, but she didn't expect them to solve her problems.

"Thank you for dinner, Liz, and everything you're trying to do, but I could no more impose on Mac and Millie than I could any of the rest of you. You're all newly married with plans and dreams of your own."

Cassie got to her feet, having been at their new ranch house too long already. Liz still had veterinarian work waiting for her. "I'll be moved into an apartment in town within two weeks. I want to get ready for the baby in a place of my own." She smiled at her. "No amount of generosity on your part will get me to change my mind."

"But you're going to let us give you a baby shower, right?"

"I'd love that!"

"Good. Then it's settled. I'll talk with the others to plan a date and call you."

Thankful she had her own transportation, Cassie was able to leave so Liz and Connor could enjoy the rest of the evening. After leaving the Bannock ranch, she drove to White Lodge and bought a pot of white mums at the supermarket. From there she went to the cemetery at the northeast end of town.

Logan's grave was in the newer section. It would be several years before the planted trees grew to a significant size. She pulled up near his flat marker and got out of the truck with the flowers. One day when she had enough money, she would have a granite stone erected.

She walked over and knelt down to put the pot at the bottom of the marker. "I haven't been here for two weeks, Logan. Forgive me. So much has happened since my last visit. We're going to have a little girl, but I bet you already know that. Sam's son, Trace, is home from Italy to sell the property, so I'll be moving to town within the next two weeks.

"The family wants me to live with Liz's parents. Can you believe how wonderful they all are to me? But I could never do that to them. I've got to make my own way. It was always you and I against the world. Now it's our daughter and I facing it without you. In four months I'll be a mother."

Tears welled in her eyes. "I promise to tell her all about her wonderful daddy and keep your pictures around her forever. I'm praying that by the time she's born, Zane will have found out who shot you and can rule it an accident." She shuddered. "For so many reasons I don't want to hear it was Ned." She started crying and buried her face in her hands.

"I've asked Connor to take care of the sale of the horses. Trace said you did a beautiful job on the house. He's planning to move to Colorado to be a flight instructor for the Air Force. I love the house so much I—I just know it will sell fast. We were so happy there."

Tears dripped everywhere. "While our dream lasted, you were such a marvelous husband to me. I loved every second we were together. I'm having a hard time leaving our little house in the forest. I've taken dozens of pictures inside and out so our little girl will know how happy we were there.

"Trace asked me what you and I had decided to name her. I told him neither of us knew I was pregnant before you died. Since we don't know who your parents were, I can't name her after someone from your family's side. I'll just have to keep thinking about it. One day the right name will come to me." She wiped the tears off her face and got to her feet. "Goodbye for now, Logan."

She turned and started for the truck. Evening had fallen. But this time as she left the cemetery, everything was different from all the other times because Cassie felt as if she'd reached the end of an era. All the way back to the ranch she thought of the new troubling era looming before her.

Trace owned the home she'd been living in. When she arrived at the house, he would be there instead of Logan. He'd been the first person to see the ultrasound picture of the baby and ask the baby's name. Besides her cousins, he'd been the one and only man to take her to a movie or anywhere since the funeral.

Cassie had been preparing Trace's meals, doing his wash. He'd walked and ridden the horses with her while they'd talked about the intimate, private issues of their lives. They'd been thrown together so hard and fast, it felt as if they'd skipped the normal period of getting acquainted. Last night during a heated conversation she'd actually accused him of sounding like a husband. To think she would even entertain the thought seemed like a betrayal of Logan's memory.

When she pulled to a stop in front of the ranch house and saw that Trace's car was gone, Cassie resented the fact that she even noticed. What was worse—for that infinitesimal moment, she experienced disappointment. What did that mean?

It means you need to move out of there pronto, Cassie Dorney. Two weeks couldn't come soon enough.

The second she'd showered, she got into bed and went to sleep. When she awakened late Wednesday morning, she had no idea when Trace had returned or if or when he'd gone to bed. Once she'd dressed in fresh maternity jeans and a blouson-type blouse, Cassie went to the kitchen for a glass of juice and some toast. She found a note from Trace sitting on the kitchen table.

> Good morning, Cassie. Just wanted you to know that I've gone to town for some supplies. I'll be back by eleven. The Realtor Bud Hawksworth and a potential buyer will be coming to the ranch around noon.

> T.

A buyer already?

At the mention of the ranch being sold, there went that pain again. Not only her pain, but pain for Sam Rafferty, too. He had to be broken up over his son's intention to live in Colorado. It wasn't just because the property was going to pass into other hands, but because he'd wanted this for Trace's legacy.

Cassie appreciated Trace giving her warning and hurried through the house to be sure everything was clean and in order. After she'd fixed her breakfast and had eaten, she went out to the barn and led the horses to the paddock. While they enjoyed the morning sun, she mucked out their stalls, put fresh hay in the nets and made certain there was fresh water.

Once that chore was done, she went back to the house for the basket and spent the rest of her time picking any ripened strawberries. She didn't want anything left undone.

Her watch said it was close to eleven when she heard a car pull up to the house. Her heart raced to realize Trace was home even sooner than she'd expected. While she was coming to the end of the last row, she heard men's voices behind her and turned around.

"Sorry to startle you, Mrs. Dorney. I'm Bud Hawksworth and this is Mr. Walker. Did Trace tell you we were coming?"

The Realtor wore a summer suit and glasses. "Yes, but he's not here yet."

"Mr. Walker's plane landed early so we've come ahead of time. I told him you've been looking after the place since your husband passed away. I'm very sorry to hear about your loss."

Mr. Hawksworth had taken a liberty coming early, one Cassie thought inappropriate. She took a steadying breath. "Thank you."

"The exterior of the house is charming and so unexpected. Mind if we walk around until Trace gets here?"

"I guess that's all right."

"We'll take a look at the barn. Maybe the horses he mentioned are for sale, too?"

"They're my horses," she murmured, disliking the way Mr. Walker was eyeing her.

"I see."

To her chagrin the other man said, "You go on, Bud. I'll catch up with you in a minute." The potential buyer was probably in his late forties and somewhat attractive with blond hair and burnished skin. In khaki shorts and a T-shirt, his lean build reminded her of a golfer. "Your garden is thriving. Looks like you're going to have raspberries soon."

"One hopes."

"How long have you worked here?"

"A year."

"Then you know all its secrets."

She didn't care for the way his brown gaze seemed to leer at her. "Like all hundred-year-old properties, it needs constant upkeep, as Mr. Rafferty will tell you."

"If I buy this place, I'll need someone to take care of it when I'm not here."

Cassie knew what the offensive man was getting at. He could see she was pregnant, but her condition didn't make a difference to him. "That's something for you to take up with Mr. Hawksworth. If you'll excuse me."

She headed for the house with the basket, aware of his roving eyes on her retreating back. There was nothing she detested more than a man who looked at her as if he was undressing her. It sickened her. He obviously had money or he wouldn't be wasting the Realtor's time. But already she was hoping Trace wouldn't sell to him.

As for the horses, Cassie wouldn't let such a disgusting man get near them. She marched into the house in a mood and ran right into Trace, who must have been on his way out the back door. As the basket dropped, a small cry escaped her lips. He grasped her upper arms.

"I'm sorry, Cassie."

"I'm the one who needs to apologize." She tilted her head back to look at him. Their faces were so close, she felt his warm breath on her lips and had to stifle a moan. "I wasn't watching where I was going."

"You're upset. I can feel you trembling. What's happened? I saw another car out there."

"Mr. Hawksworth came early with Mr. Walker."

"So I see. And?"

"It's nothing."

"The hell it isn't," he muttered in a deep voice.

Reeling from his touch, she eased out of his arms and reached for the basket. Luckily it hadn't tipped over. She put it on the counter. "They're waiting for you, Trace. While you show them around, I've got some errands to run."

It was the best excuse she could come up with at the spur of the moment. She knew he wanted an explanation, but she couldn't tell him the whole truth. Otherwise he'd find out she didn't want him to sell the ranch, never mind that it was none of her business. And what would he think if she said Mr. Walker reminded her of a predator? Trace would decide she was as unstable as her brother.

She dashed out of the kitchen and down the hall to her room for her purse. Once again as she started to leave, Trace blocked the doorway, but this time they didn't collide. He looked good in his Western shirt and jeans. Better than good. All of him looked so-o good.

"I'm not going outside until you tell me what happened."

She let out a sigh, resigned that she needed to say something to appease him. "I have an idea he'd like me to work for him if you sell him the ranch."

"What else?" he demanded. Emotion had turned his eyes a darker blue.

"There's nothing else."

"Cassie—"

"Oh, all right. It was just the way he looked at me. It made me shudder." Cassie could tell when a man found her attractive, but not in an offensive way. This man's probing gaze was something else. "Maybe I could be wrong, so please don't let that color your judgment."

His body tightened. "Say no more."

"Trace—"

But he'd bolted down the hall and out the back door. She'd done it now. Part of her thrilled to his protective instincts. The other part felt terrible if it meant the sale he needed wouldn't go through because of something she'd said. She should have left the ranch after seeing to the horses. But there was nothing holding her back now!

Grabbing her purse, she rushed through the house and flew out the door to her truck. She was so shaken, she knew her blood pressure had to have spiked. What she needed was something to calm her down.

When she reached town and drove by the Clip and Curl beauty salon, she decided a visit there would be therapeutic. After turning around she parked in front. You could walk in and wait for someone to wait on you. The place was bursting with customers of course. The red-headed owner, Mildred Paxton, sat behind her counter.

"Hey, Cassie— I haven't seen you in ages. You're pregnant! I didn't know."

"Neither did I until after Logan died."

"You look wonderful. How do you feel?"

"Frazzled. I need pampering, but this place is so busy I'll come back later."

"No, no. I'll do your hair myself."

"Really?"

"For a favorite customer, anytime. What do you want?"

"A shampoo and style."

"Come on over to my chair."

In a minute Cassie was draped in a smock. For someone else to do her hair was the height of luxury. "My kingdom to have my hair washed every day by you. This is heavenly, Mildred."

"I hear you."

"How's your daughter?"

"Rosie's fine, but her husband had to move to Billings so I've lost my helper. You don't know anyone who's looking for a part-time job, do you?"

Cassie gripped the sides of the chair. "What kind of work?"

"Running the desk, making appointments, taking the money. I usually come in at three to finish up the day, but so far no takers. Everyone wants full-time work. I don't blame them." Mildred finished the rinse and wrapped her hair in a towel.

When Cassie sat up she said, "I might know someone who could do it until her baby's born."

The older woman stared at her. "You need a job."

She nodded. "For the next four months. After the baby gets here, I'll need it more than ever." No one needed to know Trace's plans for the ranch. "I'll be out of a job in another month."

"I don't get it. You're a Bannock."

"Every Bannock I know works hard." Except for Ned who treated work as a joke.

"You know what I mean, Cassie. For you to work in the salon…"

Cassie had met with this kind of mind-set before. "Tell you what, Mildred. I've put out feelers for work in several places. Even with a college degree, it hasn't helped produce results yet. If nothing pans out by morning, do you mind if I call you for an interview?"

"You're serious!"

"I am. I did the accounts, took money and handled reservations for hunters while Logan and I ran the Rafferty ranch. I'm friendly with quite a few of your regular customers. This job would be perfect since I'm an early morning person. By late afternoon I can go home and put my feet up the way the doctor told me to."

"Tell *you* what. I won't hold my breath because I can't imagine you not getting snapped up by someone else. This job doesn't pay that well."

"But you'll give me a chance if I phone you tomorrow? Provided you haven't found someone else?"

"We'll see. Between now and tomorrow anything can happen."

At least Mildred hadn't said no.

After she left the beauty salon, Cassie went to the drive-through for a hamburger and a lemonade. On her way back to the ranch she felt energized after her talk with Mildred, who'd done a great job on her hair. If she hired Cassie and she could move into that apartment soon, she would have solved all her problems for a while.

Trace was at the root of her guilty turmoil. Earlier today when he'd grasped her arms, she'd felt desire for him arc through her body again more intense than at the lake. To experience such a yearning this soon after Logan's death filled her with sorrow over her weakness. She couldn't allow it to go on happening.

Once she was out of Trace's house for good and they

didn't have to see each other again, maybe she could forget how he made her feel.

When she reached the house, his Explorer was gone. Thankful for the respite she hurried inside, eager to get busy and put up the last of the strawberries. But when she walked into the kitchen and read the note Trace had left on the table, she had to sit down so she wouldn't fall.

Cassie—

I should never have left you alone when I knew Bud was coming over. It won't happen again. For your information, Mr. Walker has been told I'm looking for a family man who plans to be a full-time rancher.

Can I count on you to hold down the fort for a while? After hearing from Nicci again, I've decided nothing can be resolved over the phone so I'm flying to Italy and talk to her face-to-face. I don't know how soon I'll be back, but with you in charge I have no worries.

The guys know my plans and they'll check in on you to make certain you're all right. If there's any problem at the ranch, call my father and he'll take care of it. My main concern is you. Please take very good care of yourself and that baby.

T.

Cassie sat there in a daze. What was it Mildred had said? Anything can happen between today and tomorrow. She struggled for breath. Trace was on his way to Monfalcone. *He's in love with Nicci.* From the looks of it, he would be married before long and probably live in Italy after all.

Whatever feelings Cassie struggled with, they were on her part, not his.

She ran to the bedroom and buried her face in the pillow, heedless of her pregnancy or her new hairdo. His note had left her in complete limbo.

THE WHITE TORNIELLI villa gleamed in the sun. One of the staff told Trace he'd find Nicoletta by the pool. He wanted to surprise her and made his own way beneath the purple bougainvillea overhanging the portico to the deck.

He found her lounging in a minuscule black bikini. She wore sunglasses and was talking on the phone, probably to her friend Bianca. If she was in pain, it didn't sound that way to him. She hadn't seen him yet. After a month's separation, the sight of her playing with the strands of her black hair should have excited him. She was at once so familiar to him.

All that animation bequeathed from the genes of her dynamic family was in evidence. Nicci was a beautiful creature of her unique environment. But Trace had been away from her and removed from this world for quite some time. He knew in his gut that to take her out of it would kill the part of her that was so scintillating. The part that had drawn him to her.

The fact that she still couldn't bring herself to fly to the United States meant she understood herself well and had done both of them a great favor. Their separation had given her second sight, too. Unless he came to her and melted into her world, they wouldn't work.

"Nicci?"

She turned her head and threw off her sunglasses. *"Caro!"* But she didn't come running yet. Instead she got up off the lounger and took in his Western shirt, jeans and cowboy boots. Her dark brown eyes played over him. "I don't recognize you like this. You've turned into a Montana cowboy." Her strong Italian accent made her words sound so charming in English.

"I'm afraid this is the real me. For ten years I forgot."

Nicci looked lost. He couldn't blame her. "What do you mean?"

"When I joined the Air Force, I was running away from my past because I was in pain."

"Your parents' divorce did that to you."

"Yes. You've never known that kind of pain. You have an intact family. But since I've been home, my past has caught up with me. I never really wanted to leave it."

Her eyes filled. "So what are you saying?" she cried. "Are you glad that laser almost blinded you?"

"With hindsight I can say yes because it brought me to my senses sooner. I've come to tell you that I've decided not to take the position at the Air Force Academy. Ranching is what I love to do." When he realized what Lamont Walker planned to do with his property, Trace had had an epiphany. He didn't want anyone living there but him. "If you could live with me on the ranch and like it, then I could see us getting married because I love you, Nicci."

She shook her head. "I love you, too, but I don't want that kind of life, *Caro*."

"I know, and I respect you more than you can imagine for being totally honest with me. Our happiness depends on it. I owe you so much. That's why I'm here so we could say these things to each other in person."

"I'm remembering what you told me about your mother. She never liked being a rancher's wife."

"It's true. Ranch life isn't for everyone." But there was one person he knew who loved that life.

Visions of Cassie had been in his mind from the first time he'd seen her in the garden. Though she was still in mourning for Logan, she loved every minute of her time on that ranch. She'd been born into a ranching family.

After hearing her tell him what Lamont Walker had intimated and how'd made her cringe, Trace had been more than annoyed. In truth, he'd felt like decking the guy before the two men had driven away. His feelings for Cassie had grown so strong, they refused to go away.

"As long as we're being truthful, why did you never want an engagement with me?"

"Because I knew I could never work for your father. Not that he isn't a fine man, but I have to be my own boss."

"But I'm talking before your injury, *Caro*."

"Maybe because of my parents' history, in my subconscious I was afraid of commitment."

"What are we going to do?" came her plaintive cry.

"Marriage isn't the answer for us, Nicci."

"But I can't bear to lose you. I'll get dressed and we'll go to your hotel."

"I didn't check into one."

"Why?"

"Because I didn't think it would be a good idea."

"Since when? Something about you has changed." She moved closer and slid her arms around his neck. "Kiss me, *Caro*. It has been such a long time."

In ways it had seemed like an eternity since they'd made love. He pulled her close and kissed her, but the driving passion he'd always felt for her was missing. To his shock he found himself wishing it was Cassie in his arms. She'd been so shaken by that lowlife Bud had brought out to the ranch, Trace had wanted to kiss her until she forgot everything else and clung to him.

As gently as he could, he removed Nicci's arms from around his neck and kissed her hands. "I'll never forget you, Nicoletta Tornielli. Meeting you, knowing you, was the best thing to happen to me after I was deployed here. You brought happiness into my life when I didn't think it could be found. I wanted to marry you, but our dream wasn't meant to be. You have to know I enjoyed every minute of it. Now I have to go. A taxi's waiting for me."

She looked stung by his words. "You planned to leave so soon?"

He nodded. "We both know it has to be this way."

"After flying all that distance, why are you in such a hurry to get away from me?"

"This is difficult enough without prolonging it, don't you think? Do we really want to make things harder on ourselves?"

A silence surrounded them. "You've met someone," she accused quietly, summoning his guilt.

"Nicci..."

"You have! I can feel it. Who is she?"

This was one time he wished Nicci didn't have such an intuitive nature. "Give my best to your family. They're wonderful people. As for you, I want your happiness more than anything in the world."

The tears trickled down her cheeks. "You haven't answered me."

"Goodbye, Nicci." He kissed her cheek.

Her perceptive comment trailed him as he headed for the portico and hurried outside to the taxi. Contrary to what he'd thought, driving away from Nicci and the villa wasn't the traumatic experience he'd expected. Trace's mind went over his session with Dr. Holbrook.

His expert advice to straighten things out with Nicci first had cleared Trace's emotional vision. Instead of more pain at seeing her again, he was filled with a sense of wonder over the relief he felt that this chapter in his life had come to an end. A whole new world awaited him back in Montana. A familiar world he'd tried to put behind him during his time in the Air Force, but he hadn't succeeded.

You're going home, Trace.

On his way to Montana, he'd make a stop in Colorado Springs to let the brass know he wouldn't be taking the teaching position after all. Once that was done, he'd head for Oregon to see his mother. Dr. Holbrook told him he needed to get rid of his anger for past hurt if he really wanted to heal, more advice Trace intended to take.

Then he'd return to White Lodge and have a big talk with his father. It was long past time Trace begged his forgiveness for being so blind.

What an irony that it took his eye being scarred by a laser to see what had been right in front of him all the time.

On Wednesday he flew into Billings, realizing he'd been gone a week. His feelings were so different from the first time he'd looked out the window two weeks ago, he couldn't believe he was the same person. The excitement missing before was in full evidence now. He picked out familiar landmarks that told him he was home. Everything he held dear was down there. Everyone...

Once he'd landed and gathered his suitcase, he picked up his car in the long-term parking and headed for White Lodge. He'd phoned his father from Portland and had asked him to meet him at the ranch at two in the afternoon. It was important.

Sam was already there on the front porch of the house reading a magazine, no doubt the latest veterinarian medical journal. Cassie's car was gone. Knowing her, as soon as his dad told her Trace would be arriving, she'd taken off so she wouldn't impose. For once he was glad she wasn't there. This gave him private time with his father.

He pulled to a stop and levered himself from the front seat. His dad got up from the swing. Trace took the porch steps in one leap and embraced his father. Tears smarted his eyelids.

A surprised laugh came out of Sam before he let him go. "What's this all about? A goodbye hug because you've decided to marry Nicci and live in Italy? Is that why she isn't with you?"

"Dad? We've got a lot to talk about."

"That's what I thought," he murmured, sounding defeated.

"You have no idea what I'm going to tell you. Sit down and I'll explain."

When his father did his bidding, Trace perched on the porch railing opposite him, too full of energy to sit. "I went to see Mother before I flew here. She sends her love."

His dad's head lifted. "How is she?"

"Good. I asked her to forgive me for being so angry with her over the divorce."

His dad sat back in obvious surprise. "That must have been quite a conversation."

"It was cathartic for both of us."

"Nothing could please me more than to hear that." He wiped his eyes.

"Not even if I told you I flew to Colorado Springs to tell them I'm not going to take that job after all?"

"You mean you're going to work for Nicci's father in Monfalcone."

"No, Dad. I mean I've come home for good. I don't want to sell the ranch. I want to work it and run cattle again, put in some crops."

One sandy brow lifted. "Is Nicci okay with that?"

"We're not getting married and we've said our goodbyes."

"What?" He was clearly in shock.

"You heard me. Oddly enough it was something she said when she saw me walk out to the pool that reaffirmed my own feelings. It proclaimed the end of our relationship because in her heart she knew a marriage between us wouldn't work."

"What did she say?"

"Nicci took one look and exclaimed, 'I don't recognize you like this. You've turned into a Montana cowboy.' Her soul was speaking to my soul, Dad.

"The truth is, I went into the Air Force because of anger over the breakup of the family. But the cowboy was always there. When I came home two weeks ago, I fought its pull. But I discovered these Rafferty roots grow so deep, you can't get rid of them. I'm here to stay. Can you ever forgive me for taking my anger out on you?"

"Oh, son..." He got up from the swing and gave Trace the biggest bear hug of his life. In a tug of war, his father always won. "Welcome home."

Both of them had to wipe their eyes. "Do you know where Cassie is?"

"She's at work."

Trace did a double take. "What work?"

"She got a part-time job at the beauty salon Mildred Paxton owns in White Lodge."

He couldn't believe it. "I didn't know she was a beautician, too."

"Oh, no. She runs the counter and makes appointments. It's only two blocks from that apartment she plans to move into. I believe it will be ready in another week. That girl is a go-getter if I ever saw one. She's up early to see to the horses before getting to the shop at nine."

"What are her hours?" Trace was stunned how fast she made decisions.

"Nine to three. She'll be home pretty soon unless she has other plans. Speaking of getting home, I've got to tell Ellen the wonderful news. We're going to have to celebrate!"

Chapter Seven

Cassie was happy to see Mildred come in through the back door of the shop. It was close to three-thirty. The owner was running late. Normally it wouldn't matter, but today Cassie wanted to get to a couple of yard sales before everything was already picked over. She was looking for a playpen in good condition.

"Sorry I got held up."

"No problem, Mildred."

"How are things?"

"Just fine!"

"How do you stay so cheerful when we both know most days it's a royal pain?"

"Not to me."

"You're so great at this job I hope you never leave. Now go on home and relax."

"Thanks, Mildred. See you tomorrow."

Cassie had parked out in the back alley. She was glad the owner was pleased with her work. So far it had gone smoothly on her new routine. She'd taken her doctor's advice and went home every afternoon to put her feet up and check her emails or watch television.

She ate the second half of a peanut butter sandwich while she drove to the first yard sale. But she didn't even get out of the cab because there weren't any baby items. Cassie would probably end up having to buy a new one. Still, there was one more sale she'd seen advertised and drove by it.

A painted wood high chair caught her eye, but after seeing all Sadie's new paraphernalia, Cassie couldn't make a decision yet. The issue of safety was a factor to consider. In the end she drove back to the ranch without having made any purchases. The budget she'd allowed herself wasn't big enough for her to acquire everything she wanted. Not when she needed a couch, bed, a TV and a dozen other things first.

Functioning on autopilot at this point, she wasn't prepared to see the brown Explorer parked in front of the house. *Trace...* He was back! She was sick with excitement and afraid, too.

He'd been gone so long, maybe he'd brought Nicci with him so she could see the ranch and they could make wedding plans. If that was the case, Cassie would sleep at Avery and Zane's until she moved to the apartment.

Not wanting to walk in on them, she knocked. When no one answered she knocked harder. After no response she unlocked the door and poked her head in.

"Hello? Trace? Are you here?"

She got brave and walked in. When she passed his bedroom she saw his suitcase next to the bed. Maybe Nicci wasn't with him after all, unless she was staying with Sam and his wife. Curious at this point, she reached for two horse snacks and walked out to the barn.

Buttercup nickered from the paddock. Cassie went over to the railing. "Hi there, Buttercup." She patted her forelock and undid the wrapper so her horse could eat. She chomped it down. "Did Masala desert you?"

"We're right here."

Trace's deep voice had her spinning around. He looked down at her with a smile that reached his brilliant blue eyes. "You don't have something for Masala, do you?"

"Of course I do." She patted the horse's head and took the treat out of the paper to feed him. "There you go." He was a chomper, too. "They're noisy eaters." It made both of them laugh. "When did you get home?"

"I drove in to the ranch around two this afternoon to meet with my dad."

A dozen questions sprang into her mind. Had he come home to tell his father he and Nicci had set a wedding date? Or had he married her while he'd been in Italy? A strange pain shot through her at the thought of either possibility. "After I saw your car out in front, I thought you might have brought Nicci home with you."

"She's not coming."

At those words Cassie's heart almost failed her. What did it mean?

While she was groping for something intelligible to say, he opened the gate and walked Masala into the paddock. Once he'd removed the bridle, he patted his rump before closing the gate. He hung the bridle over the post.

"Come in the house with me. You and I need to talk.

Dad tells me you're working at the beauty salon in town. No other job offers came through while I was gone?"

"Not yet, and Mildred needed help. It's a perfect job for me while I'm pregnant."

"If you're happy, that's all that matters. How was your Fourth of July?"

"Fine. My cousins took me to the White Lodge fireworks celebration at the park. It was fun. I'm sure you would have enjoyed it."

"When I was a kid, I lived for fireworks."

"You and every male I know."

"Connor and I put on our own shows when no one else was around. Jarod helped."

"I'm not surprised."

He opened the back door for her and followed her through to the kitchen. "Why don't you sit down while I wait on you? It's hot out there and your cheeks are rosy. Want a soda?"

She wished he wouldn't make personal comments. "A lemonade sounds good."

"Your favorite drink." He handed her one and reached for a cola. His gaze panned the kitchen. "You've put up more jam. I can't believe the abundant yield from your garden."

"The weather has cooperated."

"Only with the help of a green thumb like yours."

"I used to help my mom in the garden."

Trace snagged a chair with his boot and sat down. His eyes centered on her. "You never talk about her, but I know you miss her, especially with the baby coming."

The conversation had started to border on painful

issues she'd rather not discuss. "I miss the mother I loved before she started siding with my dad in order to keep the peace with Ned. But I'd rather talk about your news." Her heart was thudding. "Did your trip to Italy help you and Nicci figure things out?"

He drained his soda and put the empty can on the table. "There isn't going to be a wedding. We're two halves of the wrong whole."

The blood hammered in her ears. Trace wasn't going to marry her? "I—I'm sorry," she stammered.

"Don't be. It would never have worked. We both knew it and avoided the mistake of getting married and then having to end it, maybe with a child involved."

Cassie drank some of the lemonade while she assimilated what he'd just told her. She must have been born with some evil gene to be happy with his news. Her mind pounced on her next question. "Have you heard from your Realtor? Does he have more buyers lined up?"

He sat back in the chair with his arms folded. "Nope. When I flew into Billings earlier today, I dropped by his office and told him I was taking the ranch off the market. It's not for sale. Ever."

Hearing that news made Cassie positively giddy. It was a good thing she was sitting down or she might have fallen over in shock. "Did you tell your father?"

"Yeah. He was pretty happy about it."

"Pretty happy—I'm surprised he didn't go into cardiac arrest."

Laughter poured out of him.

"Do you plan to rent the property, then?"

Her question caused his laughter to subside. "No."

She didn't understand. "Then, what?"

"I'm going to live here."

That did bring her out of the chair. "You mean you're not going to Colorado Springs after all?"

Trace put his hands behind his head and stared up at her. "Nope. I stopped there on my way home and told the brass I've decided to go back to ranching."

"Are you telling me the truth?" Her voice had come out more like a squeak.

He'd tipped the chair back as far as it would go before there was an accident. "Scout's honor."

"Don't tease me, Trace."

His dark brows suddenly furrowed. He jumped out of the chair. "You went pale just now. I forgot how this news would impact you, but you don't need to worry about losing your housekeeping job."

That wasn't why she'd gone pale. It was the idea that he'd come home to live and they'd see each other coming and going. "Of course I do!"

"I want you to stay on and work for me."

She clung to one of the chair backs. "With you living here, too?"

"Why not? Unless you have designs on me."

"Be serious, Trace—" she snapped. He'd hit a nerve that ran the entire length of her body.

"Better me to be your bodyguard than Mac Henson or your cousins. They're all married. Since Zane's responsibilities prevent him from serving that purpose, I'm the logical choice."

Cassie didn't understand. "What do you mean body-guard?"

"Ralph told your cousins that Ned will be coming back to the ranch tomorrow."

Her gasp filled the kitchen. She gripped the chair back tighter.

"When I was at the Golden Spur last week I bumped into Owen Pearson at the bar. He mentioned that Ned would be released shortly." Cassie groaned. "Ralph's news confirmed it."

"If our grandfather confirmed it, then it has to be true."

"Afraid so. Your name was mentioned during my strange conversation with Owen. I can tell you now that you won't be safe from harassment if you live in that apartment. We know what Ned is capable of, but we don't know what will set him off next, or what he'll do even on his medication. There's only one place for you, here where I can protect you."

"I'm not your responsibility, Trace."

"You are now. Dad hired you and Logan to look after the property. The shooting took place on our ranch. Now that I'm back, I want you to stay put and do the same things you've been doing. It's worked so far, hasn't it?"

"Yes! Because you were in Italy and I thought you were moving to Colorado."

"Cassie—my father thinks the world of you and doesn't want anything to happen to you or the baby. This isn't just my idea."

Incredulous she said, "You mean Sam approves of us living under the same roof?"

"Yes, and your cousins will all be for the idea, too. They don't want you to be on your own either."

She shook her head. "I couldn't consider it."

One dark brow lifted. "Because of what other people will say?"

Adrenalin surged through her veins. "It's because *I* don't believe it's right!"

"Not even to protect your unborn child?"

She closed her eyes tightly for a minute. "After I move to the apartment I'll figure out a way to keep us safe."

"How?"

"If I decide it's necessary, I'll buy a handgun and take lessons out at the shooting range like Avery. You know what they say about an ounce of prevention. It's something I'll talk over with her and Zane the next time we're together."

"That's not going to stop your brother if he gets it into his mind to stalk you." Cassie shuddered. "You're in a unique and dangerous situation. The father you should be able to go to isn't there for you."

"How many times do I have to tell you this isn't your problem?" she asked in frustration.

"What if I want it to be?"

"That's because you're like your father and play the Good Samaritan even when your world has been turned upside down. You shouldn't be worrying about anything but your own affairs."

"Are you afraid of me, Cassie?"

"Of course I'm not."

"Do you trust me?"

"What a question to ask."

"Do you?" he persisted. "Because you'd be foolish to move into town, let alone move to another part of the state, when you're this far along. There'd be no one to lean on. It would make no sense. Let all of us help you. We're in this together. Everyone has a vested interest in shutting Ned down. He's been a menace to you, Jarod, Zane and now Connor."

Fear pierced her. "What has he done to him I don't know about?"

"It's what he plans to do to antagonize your cousin that has us worried. Owen told me they're going into the feral stud farm business."

"Ned?"

Trace nodded.

"That's the biggest joke I ever heard, but I know you're not joking. He's always been in competition with Connor. Whatever my cousin did, Ned tried to do and failed miserably, especially at steer wrestling. He'll probably steal some wild horses which is against the law."

"Or try to put Connor out of commission like he did Jarod."

She let out a cry. "I just can't believe he's coming home this soon. It's a nightmare."

"It doesn't have to be if you'll let me help you. Jarod assumes they're planning to use Ned's money from his recent inheritance for their latest scheme. But he says Owen's dad would never allow him to set up business on his ranch."

"I don't know. Owen has walked over his father all his life."

"Sounds like Ned and Owen are two of a kind."

"Like two peas in a pod."

"Your cousins are worried that if Ned is thwarted on that score, he and Owen will think of some other scheme that will be up to no good."

"Dad shouldn't have released that money. If my Grandfather Tyson were still alive, he wouldn't allow it. All my father does is placate Ned. There's something wrong with him, too!"

"Is your father still in counseling?"

"He was in the beginning. Unfortunately I don't know anything at this point."

"That's why Zane and your cousins are so concerned. Let's not worry about that right now. Why don't you go in the living room and put your feet up while I cook us dinner. Any suggestions? I won't use salt."

When Trace was around, he watched out for her constantly, endearing himself to her in ways he didn't realize, but this was his home. He could do what he wanted and shouldn't have to look after her, too. "There's some hamburger in the freezer."

"Great. I'll thaw it and make spaghetti. How does that sound?"

"Sure. I haven't had it in a long time," she said before leaving the kitchen. But food wasn't on her mind. Trace had given her so much to think about, she felt like she was on an emotional seesaw.

After taking a shower, she dressed in a pair of maternity jeans and a short-sleeved top in a tiny pink print on white. Bed sounded so good, she lay down on her side. Two things he'd said stood out above all else. He wasn't getting married, and he wanted to get back to ranching.

Cassie still had a hard time believing any of it. She'd thought Nicci would go to the ends of the earth for a man like Trace. Was he in pain that she couldn't bring herself to come and see where he'd lived? Even if he was certain a marriage with Nicci wouldn't work, his heart had to be aching.

She closed her eyes. His insistence that she continue to live in the house was out of the question. Cassie had made her plans and wouldn't change them. As for her brother, she didn't want to think about him coming home tomorrow. It was only a possibility that he'd killed Logan. Without proof, maybe they were all being too paranoid. The doctor wouldn't release Ned unless he felt the therapy and medications were working.

Cassie didn't like to think of her brother confined to a facility for the rest of his life if it wasn't absolutely necessary. Her parents had suffered over Ned for so many years. But when she remembered what he'd done to Jarod, and his cruelty to her and Logan, she shivered and refused to think about it.

For now she was happy to know that Trace had made peace with his past. Sam had to be euphoric that his long-lost son had found his way back home. While she lay there pondering this afternoon's unexpected events, she felt a flutter in her stomach. At first she thought it could be a hunger pain, but when it came again and again, she knew it was her baby moving.

Her heart leaped for joy. There was no other feeling like it. The sensation could be a butterfly's wing brushing against your skin, but on the inside. At her ultrasound, the doctor had told her she'd probably feel something pretty soon.

She felt beneath her top to put her hand against the bare skin of her tummy. For a few minutes she lay there absorbing the flutters that meant her daughter was alive and getting ready to be born. Pregnancy was a miracle. Full of hormones, she broke down sobbing in happy tears.

Just then Trace knocked on her door. "Cassie? Dinner's ready."

She sniffed. "Thank you."

"You sound different. I know I upset you."

"I—I'll be there in a minute," her voice faltered.

"Something's wrong. Are you in pain?"

"No."

"I can hear you crying. If anything has happened to that baby because of me, I'd never forgive myself."

"You don't understand."

"Do you need a doctor?" He sounded panicked. "Whether you're decent or not, I'm coming in."

Before she could get into a sitting position on the bed, he opened the door. One look at her lying there and he said, "I'm calling 9-1-1."

"No—" she exclaimed. "I'm crying because I felt the baby move for the first time."

In an instant the lines in his face disappeared. "You did?"

She nodded. "It's beyond incredible. I was so afraid something was wrong because I'm almost twenty-two weeks along and should have felt movement by now. But I'm getting lots of it at the moment."

He stood in the doorway watching her. "What does it feel like?" When she told him, the most tender smile she'd ever seen broke out on his face. "I'm not often around a pregnant woman."

Cassie smiled. "Being a former Ace, why doesn't that surprise me?" Motivated by a force she hardly understood herself, she told him to come over to the bed. "Give me your hand." He hunkered down so she could place it against her belly. Their faces weren't that far apart. "Just wait a minute and you'll feel it." Their eyes studied each other. "She senses a male presence."

"You think she knows the difference?"

"Not only your touch, but your voice. She heard it when I showed you her first photograph. Move your hand a little. Maybe that will stimulate her."

Trace's touch was stimulating Cassie so much, she could hardly breathe. "There—did you feel that?"

A look of wonder broke out on his face. "Like the merest whisper."

"That's exactly what it's like."

Another minute of amazing sensations they could both feel passed before he suddenly took his hand away and got to his feet, breaking the intimacy they'd shared. "Thank you, Cassie. That's one experience I'll never forget."

BOMBARDED BY NEW EMOTIONS, Trace strode through the house and out the back door to get a grip while he put the horses in the barn. Since seeing the sonogram, he'd almost felt as if he was the father of Cassie's baby. For those precious moments just now, he'd forgotten he *wasn't* the father. Was there any woman alive sweeter than Cassie? More generous?

But in his line of vision Logan Dorney's face in the framed picture had stared back at him, bringing him to his senses. Naturally she kept his photograph on the table next to her bed. That was the first time he'd seen her husband. He was attractive and had a clean-cut look in the dressy Western shirt he'd worn for the picture.

Because of a fatal gunshot wound, the man would never see the fruition of his efforts in the garden. He would never see the little baby growing inside Cassie. He'd never hold his wife in his arms again.

When Trace had felt the evidence of new life inside Cassie, a primitive need had been born inside him to protect her and the baby at all cost.

She was on the phone in the kitchen when he went back inside a little later. He served up two plates of spaghetti with bread and butter. Knowing what her doctor said, he gave her ice water while he drank coffee. After she hung up, she joined him at the table to eat. The sparkle in her eyes was back.

"That was Avery. She called to plan a baby shower for me. When I told her your latest news, she was so thrilled she's decided to have a big barbecue on Saturday night. It will be your welcome-home party, plus a shower. She'll invite your father and Ellen and anyone else you'd like to be there."

"Everyone I care about will already be on her list."

Starting with the gorgeous female seated across the table from him.

"So is Saturday night okay for you? You're supposed to let her know."

He finished his coffee and pulled out his cell phone. "I'll call her now to thank her. I have no plans for Saturday night." *I'm not going anywhere.*

THE LIVING ROOM of the Corkin ranch house was packed. Everyone had turned out to welcome Trace home. After the feast out on the patio, Zane and Avery had assembled the crowd inside so Cassie could open her shower gifts.

"It's time for bed, Ryan."

"I don't want to."

"Come on, honey." Sadie had already put her baby down with a bottle in the guest bedroom, but Zane's nephew was fighting going to sleep, not willing to miss out on the fun.

"Auntie Cassie?" He ran over to her. "Mommy says you and Trace are going to have a baby. I want to see all the presents."

Trace was sitting across the room from her, but he didn't miss the blush that filled her cheeks. She'd worn an attractive khaki skirt with a cream-colored cotton knit sweater that blended with her golden-blond hair. "I'm having a baby, but Trace isn't the daddy."

"How come?"

"You remember Logan?"

"Um, I think."

Jarod saved the moment and swept him up in his arms. "Come on, Tiger. It's way past your bedtime."

"I hope it's a boy like Cole," he said over Jarod's shoulder.

"I'm afraid it's going to be a girl."

"A girl—" He frowned, causing everyone to laugh, including Trace. "What's her name?"

"I haven't decided yet."

Jarod carried him out of the room before he could say anything else. Trace loved it. He'd loved every moment of tonight and it wasn't over.

Avery and Liz started the gift giving. By the end of the evening, Cassie had everything she'd need for the well-dressed, well-equipped baby. By the time it was over, she was in tears. The guys cleaned up the mess before carrying everything to Trace's car. Pretty soon people were saying good-night.

While they'd been inside, a wind had started up that hadn't been present during the barbecue. The weatherman had forecast some rain, but it wouldn't hit until later. Cassie walked out of the house holding Ralph's arm while Connor held the other.

Trace's father and Ellen followed. They headed for Jarod's car, parked next to Trace's. "I wish your Grandpa Tyson had been here tonight."

"So do I," she murmured and kissed Ralph's cheek. "I'm so thankful you're alive and could be here. Thank you for your gift. To start a college fund for my daughter is beyond wonderful."

"No one deserves it more, and I wouldn't have missed tonight for the world." He flicked a glance to Trace, who was holding the front passenger door of Jarod's car open for him. "The good Lord brought you back to us, Trace. Now that you're home, be sure you take good care of my Cassie. She and her baby are mighty precious to me."

Trace smiled at her. "I will if she'll let me."

Ralph looked at her. "Of course you will. I don't want to hear about you living in town in some apartment. You stay put, young lady." Jarod's exact words to Trace.

"I'm afraid she's a Bannock with a mind of her own," Trace said when he could see Cassie was uncomfortable. She must have heard that a dozen times throughout the party.

"Don't you let her do it," Ralph warned in a serious tone.

Connor exchanged a wordless message with Trace before helping his grandfather into the car. They were all aware Ned was home but no one more than Ralph, who feared for Cassie.

As Trace opened his own car door for her, his father gave her a hug. "You mind Ralph, Cassie. He knows what's good for you."

"Thanks for the advice, Doc."

His father shut her door, then hugged Trace hard before leading Ellen over to their car.

Trace waved to the others and got behind the wheel, anxious to be alone with Cassie. He hadn't known this kind of contentment in years. They didn't have far to go. The weather was definitely growing more blustery, adding to the excitement at the thought of the two of them being together in his house.

He glanced over at her. "Are you tired?"

"A little, but it was such a wonderful party I don't care."

"That Ryan was the life of the party. Jarod and Sadie have their hands full with two children."

"They do, and they love it. Little Cole, or Sun in His Hair, is absolutely adorable."

"Just like your baby is going to be. I guess she can't be given a Crow name," he teased.

"Only Jarod's offspring are entitled."

"He always did love his Crow heritage. It's a shame he never got to know his mother."

"I agree. But he has everything he wants now with Sadie and the children."

Trace swallowed to get rid of the lump in his throat. "After tonight I think your child won't want for a single thing."

"No." He heard a big sigh. "Everyone was so generous, I don't know how to repay them."

"They don't expect anything. All they want is for you to be happy and safe."

"I know. I swear if one more person had told me to stay on your ranch…"

"Did their remarks upset you?"

She shook her head. "I have the dearest family and friends in the world. But they're so focused on me and what happened to Logan, they're not considering your situation."

"I don't have one, Cassie. I'm eager to get started on some projects. It would be a relief to me if you were there doing the things you always do. I could keep a better eye on you after you get off work at the beauty shop. If you move to that apartment, everyone who attended the party will be checking up on you all the time, including me. Ralph knows what goes on in his son's household with Ned and he's worried enough to warn you to be careful."

"That's what I'm afraid of, Trace. I don't want to be anyone's project."

"If you stay with me, then everyone can get on with living."

"But it's not fair to you. I'm a liability, and you're too much of a gentleman to admit it."

He scoffed. "You couldn't be more wrong. If anything I'm the intruder in your world. You were getting along just fine until I came home. Don't you know I love getting up to the smell of strawberry jam? I'm crazy about your cooking. I like walking into a clean house and I sleep better knowing someone's in the house when I go to bed. Flying can be a lonely business and I've done it for a long time."

"I've wondered about that."

"Have you ever heard of Pauline Gower?"

"No."

"She was a British pilot during WWII. She said that 'to be alone in the air at night is to be very much alone… cut off from everything and everyone. Nothing's "familiar" any longer.'"

"Is that how you felt at times?"

"Exactly like that. Another of her quotes was right on. She said that 'one feels rather like Alice in Wonderland after she has nibbled the toadstool that made her grow smaller—and like Alice, one hopes that the process will stop while there is still something left."

"Sounds like she was a writer, too."

"Yes."

"Do you miss it? Flying I mean."

"No. I didn't live for it like some pilots do. It provided an escape for me at a time when I was floundering. I wanted to get far away."

"You weren't alone, Trace. I had those same feelings at a very young age and couldn't do anything about them until I went away to college. There was a time when I swore I'd never come back. If I hadn't met Logan on a visit, I'd be living somewhere else in the state."

"Well I for one am glad you ended up right where you are."

Trace left the highway and drove along the dirt road to the ranch house. He'd left the two outside lights on. Cassie's description of the little house in the woods came to mind. "With your painted shutters at this time of night, you'd think we'd stumbled on to the Hansel and Gretel house."

A small smile appeared. "It does kind of remind you of that old fairy tale."

He parked and turned off the engine. "You don't really want to move to an apartment when you have a home here for the present. Do everyone a favor and stay until after the baby is born. By then we'll have a good idea about Ned's state of mind. It will give you time to find the kind of job you really want."

"But—"

"No buts, Cassie. Don't pressure yourself to make

a decision you might regret. Who knows? Maybe an apartment won't look good to you once the baby is here. You may want to rent a house for you and your daughter. Promise me you'll think about working for me, at least until Christmas. Then you can reevaluate."

She didn't answer him. He hoped that was a good sign.

Chapter Eight

"Come on. Let's go inside with your haul."

"That's exactly what it is!" Cassie exclaimed.

"Dad won't be staying here so why don't we store everything in his room."

"But what if he and Ellen want to sleep over one night?"

"All they'll need is the bed."

Without saying anything, she got out of the car before Trace could help her and reached for one of the sacks in back filled with baby clothes. The wind was blowing harder now.

"You must be tired after volunteering at the sanctuary earlier."

"I'm not that tired."

As his father had remarked, Cassie was a hard worker. "How's Giselle by the way?"

"As precious as ever."

"She probably waits for your visits."

"I think she's happy when I call to her."

He smiled. "You only think?"

"Everyone loves her."

"But I wager you're her favorite. I'll go by there again soon and see if she remembers me. In the meantime if you'll open the front door, I'll bring in all the rest of the things."

Trace handled the heavier boxes with furniture that had to be put together. After several trips he got everything inside the bedroom. "What did you work on today at the sanctuary?"

"We painted the new fox condo. Paul did the roof and sides while Lindsey and I worked on the legs."

"The same brown color?"

"Yes."

"Does it have shutters?"

She chuckled. "No."

"I think you should add two and apply your terrific artwork to brighten things up."

"I'm afraid it would be a little much."

"You're so expert at it, we can't let that talent go to waste. If you noticed, I didn't give you a gift at the party. Why don't you open the closet door?"

Cassie stopped emptying the bags and walked over to do his bidding. "Oh—a little wooden toy box." She leaned over and opened it. "How darling!"

"It's unfinished. I thought you could paint it and decorate it yourself."

She stood up before her eyes darted to his. "You do too much, Trace."

He hunched his shoulders. "If you don't want it—"

"You know I do! I'm just overwhelmed by your thoughtfulness. You're too generous for your own good."

"And you're too stubborn for yours." He opened the top dresser drawer. "This is empty. Shall we put the clothes in here?"

Cassie walked over to the bed and lifted a little white bodysuit from the sack. They both chuckled. "Trust Connor to find this eenie-meanie bull outfit. Look at the size of that steer's horns!"

"How about Liz's contribution?" He pulled out the little pink-and-white bodysuit dress with two cowboy boots on the front. "I can't wait to see her in this. Or this." Trace drew out another bodysuit. "Super cowgirl."

"That was Mac and Millie's contribution. I never saw so many cute baby clothes in my life." She started folding them and the receiving blankets in the drawer.

Trace never saw a cuter mother-to-be in his life. While she got busy doing that, he opened the box containing an ivory-colored crib. He had it assembled before she turned to look at him.

"You shouldn't have set that up."

"Too late. It's done. Don't you want to see what the mobile looks like attached to it? Jarod says Cole is already intrigued by his."

After a slight hesitation, she opened the box and pulled it out. He knew Cassie couldn't resist. A horse, bear, cowboy boot, dog and bull dangled from a tan cowboy hat. A laugh escaped her lips. "What won't they think up next?" She put it at one end of the crib.

"Every little well-brought-up cowgirl should have one of those." Trace took the crib mattress out of the other box and fit it inside the crib. "The padding with the cowboy boots is here somewhere." He found it and set it around. "All this crib needs now is your baby girl."

Cassie stood there clutching the crib rail with a pained expression. After such a great evening, his spirits plummeted to see it. "I realize Logan is the one you wished were here doing this with you. I'm so sorry, Cassie."

He left the bedroom and walked through the house to the back door into the wind. A ride on Masala was what he needed, and he didn't care if it started to rain on him. In practically begging Cassie to stay on at the ranch, he'd added too much pressure by erecting the crib. He should never have done that. It hadn't been on purpose, but he'd been so carried away by the events of the night, he hadn't stopped to think. She had every right to resent him. *Damn and damn.*

In a few long strides he reached the barn, but the left door was open and banged against the structure with every gust of air. Trace had closed the doors before they'd left for the party. In all the years he'd lived here, he'd never seen the wind blow one of them open. They were heavy.

Whether it had been left open on purpose or not, he was convinced someone had been here.

Walking inside, he turned on the overhead light and headed for the horses' stalls to check on them. Speaking in low tones, he examined them to make certain they were all right. They nickered back and forth while he inspected the other two empty stalls and the tack room. Nothing seemed amiss, but he wasn't convinced a force of nature had been responsible.

Without hesitation he phoned Zane who'd probably gone to bed by now. He picked up on the third ring. "Trace? What's up?"

"After the great party, I'm sorry to bother you, but this couldn't wait." In the next breath he told him what he'd discovered when he went out to the barn. "If we had an intruder over here, he could have left a fingerprint or two. I haven't touched the handle or the door."

"I'll be right over."

While he stood inside the opening to get out of the wind, Cassie came out of the house. "Trace?"

He stepped outside. "I'm right here."

"What are you doing? Why is the light on?"

"Come inside and I'll tell you. Don't touch anything."

When she reached him, her hair was in beautiful disarray. "I thought you'd gone out to the front porch."

"Actually I was going to take a ride on Masala before going to bed, but I found the barn door open the way you see it right now. Before we left tonight, I closed both of them. I could be wrong and it was just the wind, but I think we might have had an intruder while we were at the party. So I phoned Zane. He should be here in a minute to lift any prints he might find besides yours and mine."

She bit her lip. "The wind wouldn't do that unless the door had already been ajar."

"I'm inclined to agree."

Cassie left him long enough to go over to the horses. While she was talking to them, Trace saw headlights in the drive coming toward him. Zane got out of his truck with a bag. Jarod was with him.

"Thanks for coming."

"I'm going to test for fingerprints. Let's go in the house first so I can get a set of yours and Cassie's. Then I'll test for prints on the front and back door of the house, window frames and the doors of Cassie's truck before we go to the barn."

"While you do that, I'll take the barn door off the hinges and set it inside," Jarod offered. "It'll be easier to work on out of the wind."

"Good idea." Zane handed him a screwdriver from his bag before Trace and Cassie went in the house.

An hour later everything had been done and the door was put back and shut. "I'll get all this off to the crime lab in Missoula first thing in the morning. It ought to be interesting to see what they come up with. You know what this means if we find what we're looking for."

Cassie's anxious eyes revealed her fear. "Will it be enough to send him back to the facility for good?"

Jarod hugged her around the shoulders. "No question about it, cousin."

After they left, Trace walked her back in the house and locked the door. "Cassie?" he said as they reached the kitchen. "Do me a favor? Zane says he'll ask for results ASAP. If I'm right and Ned was bold enough to trespass tonight, he'll do it again once you're in that apartment. Promise me you'll stay here where I can protect you."

An odd sound came out of her. "You don't have to say anything more, Trace. When I came looking for you earlier, it was to tell you that I'll stay and work here.

"Neither Ralph or your father minced words with

me tonight. I'm not going to let my pride make everyone so nervous for me, they lose sleep over it. I've already left a voice mail with the landlord of the apartment that I won't be wanting it after all. I'm sure he'll refund the money.

"Ralph's health has been so much better since Sadie first came back, I don't want to be the one to put him in bed again. He made a promise to my Grandfather Tyson to watch out for me. No one takes responsibility more seriously than he does."

Thank heaven.

"Then you know how I feel because my father put me under the same mandate where you're concerned."

"I'm sorry, Trace."

"For what exactly?"

"For being a liability. And for the heartache you must be feeling because your marriage plans didn't go through. While you were putting the crib together, all I could think of was you, wishing this baby was yours and Nicoletta's."

That's what had put the pain in her eyes? Not the memory of Logan?

"I *was* wishing your baby was mine, Cassie," he whispered. "Yours and mine."

Her green eyes widened.

"I found myself envying your husband. If you remember a certain conversation before I left for Italy, I challenged you to stay with me, unless you had designs on me and were reticent. That was my way of teasing you. But even as a tease, you let me know in a hurry that nothing could be further from the truth. A love like yours doesn't come along every day. You left your family to be with Logan. As I've told you before. He was a lucky man."

"If Nicoletta couldn't leave her family, I can't blame her, not when she comes from such a different world. But it ruins your dreams of a family with her."

"Once the injury happened, I believe it brought both our dreams to an end. In truth, I don't think I was ever in love with her enough, or I would have done what she'd wanted and live there." He'd loved Nicci. If things had worked out differently, he might have married her and then regretted it because deep down he'd always longed for home. It would have caught up with him.

"With hindsight I can see that if you don't love someone with every fiber of your being, then how can you expect to make it through the difficult times of marriage? You and Logan had that kind of tenacity."

"It wasn't perfect. Deep inside he was insecure because he'd been orphaned. When Ned put him down to Dad, it did a lot of damage though he didn't show it in front of other people. I had to beg him to let us try for a baby. Without a role model, he was convinced he'd make a terrible parent."

"How sad."

She nodded. "He'd been in half a dozen foster homes before he turned eighteen and could be on his own. I told him it didn't matter that he didn't know his father. It was in the doing of being a father himself that he'd find out how to be a great father. We'd learn together. But it wasn't meant to be."

"Are you the one that found him in the forest?" he

whispered. Trace had wanted to know the details, but had never dared ask until tonight.

"No. When he didn't come home for dinner and it got later and later, I called your father in alarm. He in turn called my cousins and Zane. They all went out with flashlights and found him facedown near one of the streams. I told you about the dead marten that lay nearby."

"I don't know how you lived through that."

"I don't either," she laughed sadly. "Those first few weeks are a complete blank to me. Avery and the girls took turns staying with me. When I discovered I was pregnant, it was like I'd been brought back to reality and had something to live for again."

"His little girl…" He took a deep breath. "Was Logan Dorney his birth name?"

"He never knew. It was the one given to him at the orphanage in Dillon. He never did find out if they just assigned him that name, or if it was the name of one of his birth parents."

"Well he may not have known his parents, but he was married to a wonderful woman."

Tears filled her eyes. "But that so-called wonderful woman had a brother who wouldn't leave him alone." Trace saw her hands tighten into fists. "He jeered him and mocked him and—" But she couldn't go on and broke down.

Not immune to her pain, Trace pulled her into his arms and rocked her while she poured out her grief. Cassie had been holding all this in for such a long time, she had difficulty quieting down. It was past time for her to let it out. Trace was fiercely glad he was the one she'd turned to. They had a connection that was growing stronger.

When she eventually eased away from him and lifted her tear-ravaged face, it was all he could do not to protest. "The front of your shirt is wet. I'm so sorry to do that to you."

"Hey—you're pregnant and have the right to fall apart anytime you want."

Cassie laughed. A good sign that she didn't resent him. When he'd gone out to the barn earlier, he'd been convinced he'd blown it with her.

"Just call me water works. I exhibit every pregnant hormone-filled symptom in the book. I'll probably have momnesia after the baby's born, too."

"Momnesia?"

She nodded. "Pregnancy brain. They say there's forty times more progesterone and estrogen marinating in my brain right now affecting the circuits. The IQ doesn't change, but priorities do. Something about so many shelves in the brain and the top three are filled with baby preoccupation."

Trace grinned. "I learn something new every day living around you. Maybe it'll be contagious. Now I think you've had enough excitement for one day and ought to get to bed. I'll lock up and turn out the lights."

"Thank you." Her voice trembled. "For absolutely everything." She kissed the corner of his jaw and left the kitchen.

He touched his fingers to the spot where her lips had been. Next time she had one of those urges, he'd help her find his mouth.

THE NEXT FRIDAY Cassie had a dental appointment at noon. A filling had come loose and it was the only time her dentist could fit her in before he left on a trip. She called Mildred who told her to lock the salon. Rosy, her daughter, was visiting and would open it and cover the counter while Cassie was gone.

At one-thirty she returned and entered the shop through the rear door like she always did. When she reached the counter, Rosy stood up and gave her a hug.

"It's been a long time, Cassie, and you're more beautiful than ever."

"So are you."

"It isn't fair to look like you do when you're pregnant."

"Thanks for the lies. In my condition I can use them. You're really great to come in and help me out."

"Anything for an old friend. Mom says you run this place with the precision of a Swiss clock."

"Is that good or bad?"

They both laughed. "When my mom says it, you know it's good. Everything has gone smoothly. Oh—I almost forgot. You're not going to believe it. Remember Owen, your brother's old friend from high school?"

Suddenly her heart was racing like a runaway train. "Yes?"

"He came inside for a second, looked around and left. I heard he got divorced. Maybe he was looking for his ex. But don't you think that's weird? He's still that same smarmy, squinty-eyed loser."

"That doesn't surprise me." Cassie felt sick to her stomach. The news had sucked all the air out of her lungs. "Thanks for covering for me, Rosy. I'll take over now so you can get back to your mom's house."

"Let's get together the next time I'm in town."

"We'll do it."

They hugged again and she left, waving to several customers on the way out. Cassie sat down on the chair and phoned Trace.

Pick up. Please, pick up.

When it went to his voice mail she said, "Trace? I'm at the salon. After I got back from a dental appointment, Rosy said Owen Pearson came in the shop, looked around and left. I'm sure he was on some errand for Ned. You were right about my not moving to the apartment. At least here I'm surrounded by other people. Call me when you can."

The next hour got busier as it wore on, which helped keep her fears at bay. Trace had to be out doing something that kept him from phoning her back, but she knew he would when he could.

Mildred relieved her at three. Cassie chatted with her for a minute, then left through the back entrance. The first thing she noticed was the glorious sight of Trace lounging against the side of his SUV with his arms folded. Beneath his cowboy hat those shocking blue eyes filled with concern took stock of her. He straightened.

"I'd been out exercising the horses and didn't check my messages until after I'd put them back in the barn. Rather than phone you, I decided to come here and make certain you get home safely. I'll follow you, then we'll talk."

The knowledge that he was behind her filled her with relief. If she'd seen Owen skulking around the apartment, she would have been panicked. Now that there was no urgency to leave the ranch yet, she'd been sleeping so much better since Saturday night.

Though the threat of Ned was out there, she was comforted to know Trace was in the house. It seemed as though overnight he'd turned back into the rancher with new energy and plans. Cassie could tell he was happier than before. Contrary to her initial worries about living under the same roof with him, they'd slipped into a comfortable routine. By tacit agreement they respected each other's boundaries, keeping her desire for him sheathed.

She entered the house first and walked through to the kitchen. Before she could open the fridge he said, "Zane got back to me earlier today."

Cassie turned around. "What did he find out?"

"We got lucky if you can call it that. One set of prints on the inside of the barn door was a match for Owen's."

She let out a gasp.

"Zane thinks he probably got spooked and ran without securing the door and the wind did the rest. After his first arrest, he wouldn't want to be nabbed again. The police have both Owen and Ned's fingerprints on file because of the investigation into Jarod's truck accident. What we don't know is why Owen went into the barn."

"He was spying for Ned," she almost hissed. "My brother would have been furious because Masala was Logan's horse. He probably wanted to know if that horse was still in the barn now that my husband was dead. I think he plans to steal it as part of his absurd plan to run a feral stud farm."

"Ned wants to know your whereabouts, too," Trace said. "He probably heard that you are working at the beauty salon. They wanted to know your hours. It would explain Owen's brief appearance."

Cassie threw her head back. "He's up to his old tricks running surveillance for Ned. Owen does whatever Ned tells him to do. It's sick and twisted."

"I've given this a lot of thought. Ned had time to think and plan while he was in that facility. He has enjoyed harassing you over the years, but no one can predict a timetable for him to do something destructive *if* he's going to."

"Oh…he's going to. Just give him time."

"Zane and I talked about putting a restraining order on Owen, but it's Ned we want to catch in the act. To serve Owen with an order would let Ned know we're watching them. To do this right Zane feels we need to wait a little longer before netting them at the same time."

"You mean carry out a sting?"

"That's how Zane operates, but a sting takes patience. To reduce the anxiety level I have something in mind, but you'd have to be totally on board with it, too."

"What is it?"

"I was wondering how you would feel about keeping a dog around here to alert us when someone comes on the property."

His suggestion couldn't have thrilled her more. "I'd *love* a dog, Trace."

He looked pleasantly surprised. "You're not just saying that?"

"Not at all. When I was young we had a terrier, but he didn't like Ned because Ned teased him without mercy. Mother was the dog lover in the family. I begged her to give him away so Ned wouldn't hurt him. One day he was gone and mother never replaced him. I was glad, but I missed Dex horribly. He guarded me everywhere I went."

Trace's expression sobered. "Do you think Ned had something to do with his disappearance?"

"I'll never know." She turned and got a lemonade out of the fridge. "Do you want a cola?"

"Not right now, thanks."

She pulled the tab and took a long drink. "What kind of dog were you thinking of?"

Trace rested against the counter. "A sheltie."

"I adore shelties! They look like little collies."

One corner of his mouth curved upward. "Our family had a collie once named Kip."

"I bet you loved him."

"To me he was the greatest dog on earth."

"I know. I felt the same about Dex. Every dog owner feels that way, like they're another member of the family."

"Yup. Dad thinks Mr. Ogilvie's sheltie kept him alive after his wife died. He was one of my father's clients who passed away this week, leaving Dusty who was with him for eight years. His daughter lives in California. She came here to plan the funeral and sell the house. She can't take the dog with her and asked if Dad could help find a home for him."

"Oh, the poor thing." Already Cassie's heart went out to the sheltie who'd lost his owner. "No doubt he's still waiting for him to come home. I saw a documentary recently where one dog was in such great mourning, someone found it lying on the ground of its owner's tomb."

"It's a heartbreaker all right. Dad has taken care of that dog since it was a pup and knows its history. He's a blue merle with a blue eye and a brown eye."

"You're kidding—"

"Scout's honor. We could run by the Ogilvie home after dinner and see what we think."

"Why don't we go now?"

He chuckled before cocking his dark head. "Because you're supposed to put your feet up and rest."

She rolled her eyes. "Thank you for reminding me."

There was a time when she wouldn't have liked him minding her business. But in the past three weeks a change had come over her. She had to admit she loved being watched over by him. He was an amazing, caring man whose company she craved more and more.

"You're welcome. While you do that, I'll call Dad and ask him to make the arrangements for us to see the dog. I need an address."

Cassie hurried to her room and took a shower. Afterward she put on a skirt, which made a nice change from jeans, and teamed it with a summery print blouse with three-quarter sleeves. Then she lay down on the bed and propped her feet for half an hour.

Trace's suggestion that they get a dog had taken hold. She and Logan had talked about getting one when they could get their own place. It would have been so comforting to have one after he'd died, but she wouldn't have dared broach the subject to Sam. This ranch house wasn't hers.

It still isn't, Cassie.

She got up off the bed to apply lipstick and brush her hair. After putting on a mango-scented lotion, she left her room and went to the kitchen, but Trace wasn't there. She found him in the living room watching the news on TV. His black hair was still damp from the shower. He'd put on a dark blue shirt over light gray chinos. No other man could possibly match his looks or his charisma.

He got to his feet while his gaze swept over her. "You look rested. How's your appetite?"

"I'm hungry."

"So am I. Have you been to that new place called Smoky's?"

That's why he'd dressed up. "I've been meaning to try it."

"Well I'm in the mood for ribs. How about you?"

"That sounds fattening and wonderful."

"There's no fat I detect on you anywhere," he murmured. The personal comment did dangerous things to her pulse.

"Liar," she teased.

"No argument that we might be seen in town together?"

"Since I'm sure my parents know about my pregnancy by now, I'm too grateful for your help to care," she answered honestly.

A glint of satisfaction entered his eyes. He turned off the TV with the remote. "Shall we go?"

SMOKY'S TURNED OUT to be another restaurant with a Western motif and a live band of cowboys cranking out country music. The place was crowded. While they had to wait to be seated, Cassie looked so damn beautiful, Trace couldn't keep his eyes off her. Whatever fragrance she wore was heady stuff.

Less than a month ago, he'd flown into Billings at the lowest ebb of his life. If anyone had told him that in three weeks he'd be head over heels in love with Logan Dorney's pregnant wife...

At the time it would have been beyond the realm of possibility, or so he'd thought. But he knew in his gut this was the real thing. If she was compelled to live in Siberia, he'd follow her there.

The host showed them to a table and soon they were served baby back ribs with side dishes. Trace smiled at her. "They're good."

"Very tasty. Tonight I can't worry about the salt."

"Do you really notice a difference?"

"I will when I get up tomorrow. My hands and feet swell. That's why I removed my wedding ring last week." She'd done it while he'd been in Italy. "Marsha had to call 9-1-1 to get hers cut off during her pregnancy, so I'm not taking any chances."

"It was that bad?"

"It was starting to cut off her circulation. The fireman had her lie down on the kitchen table while one of them used a ring cutter that had to be inserted."

"What a painful experience."

"She said it was excruciating. Having the baby was nothing in comparison."

Trace chuckled. "I'm glad you're cautious, then. Would you like dessert?"

"Nothing more for me. I'm too full and will waddle out of here as it is, but please order some for yourself."

He shook his head. "Your strawberries are so sweet, they make the best dessert. I'll eat a bowl of them later." Trace put some money on the table to pay the bill. "Shall we leave?"

Her green eyes danced. "I thought you'd never ask."

"Too excited about the dog?" She was a true animal lover.

"I can't wait."

"Since you can't keep Giselle, maybe Dusty will be the next best thing." He stood up and helped her from her seat. They walked out to the Explorer and left for the Ogilvie home on the other side of town.

He pulled into the driveway of the small L-shaped bungalow. Before they could get out of the car, the woman came out the front door with the sheltie on a leash. Trace cupped Cassie's elbow as they walked to the front porch. They introduced themselves to the woman named Grace and expressed their sympathy for her loss.

"Thank you. You bear a certain resemblance to your father."

"I hope he doesn't mind."

Cassie laughed at him. "You know very well you take after your handsome father." Trace liked the sound of that.

Grace nodded. "I agree."

He noticed that the whole time they'd been talking, the dog stood back. "Is Dusty naturally shy?"

"Let's just say he's more reserved around strangers, but he's a dear."

"I can see that." Cassie hunkered down in front of him. "Dusty? I know you're sad to lose your best friend. How would you like to come home with us? I can tell you're a sweetie. We'd take very good care of you."

Connor had told Trace that Liz was a horse whisperer. As he watched the way Cassie talked to the dog, he sensed she had that special gift, too. The dog's ears pricked up. Like the little fox, Dusty's head moved with the sound of her voice. It was touching beyond belief.

"Do you mind if I pat your head?" She put her hand out palm down and let Dusty smell her before she scratched his ears. "We'd like to take care of you if you'll let us."

Dusty lifted his head and licked her wrist.

Trace hunkered down next to her. "What do you think, Dusty? Will you let us be your friend?" The dog cocked his head.

Cassie said, "His name is Trace, and I'm Cassie. Do you know what? I think you have a smile on your face and your blue eye looks like Trace's eyes. It's as if you belong together. Isn't that amazing?"

The dog made a little moaning sound as if he understood. His tail waved slowly back and forth.

Grace was beaming. "I'd say you've already won Dusty over. He's usually hand shy. My father would be in tears if he knew."

Cassie's eyes were full as she stood up. She looked at Trace. "What do you think?" she whispered wearing her heart in her expression.

He got to his feet. "Grace? Will you hand me the leash? Cassie and I will walk him around the front yard and see how he does."

"Come on, Dusty." The dog went with them, but after a few seconds he worked himself between them and they chuckled. When Trace made a turn, Dusty barked.

"Dusty's afraid you're going to take him back in the house," Grace called to him. "He loves walks and rides in the car."

"Do you love walks?" Cassie leaned over and rubbed his head and ears. "So do I."

This time the dog licked her everywhere he could.

"I think we'll take this dog with us, Grace. I'll get his dish and dog bed." Trace handed the leash to Cassie.

"Don't forget the toys," Cassie reminded him. "We'll wait right here for you."

Before long Trace came outside with the dog's things. Dusty walked right over to him smelling everything. When Trace opened the rear door, Cassie got in first and Dusty followed. He sat on the seat next to her. There was no question Cassie had already bonded with him.

With a smile, Trace walked around and put everything on the floor in the front before getting behind the wheel. "I told Grace not to come out in case it created more anxiety."

"That was smart."

"Are you buckled up?"

"Oh—I forgot. We're ready now, aren't we, Dusty." He barked.

When they got back to the ranch, Trace set up the dog's bed in one corner of his room with a couple of his toys. Grace had given him the doggie treats she had left, along with his bag of food and bowl.

He and Cassie took a couple of the treats out in front and exercised him to wear him out. When it was time for bed, Trace gave him a treat. "It's outside time." He walked around the side of the house to train him where to go.

"Good dog," Cassie patted him.

They went in the house and removed the leash. Dusty took off running everywhere and sniffing everything, causing them to laugh. Trace eyed Cassie. "One day your little girl is going to be able to crawl around and explore. This dog is going to break you in."

"I'm already picturing it."

Trace walked through to the kitchen. After he filled one of the bowls with water, he put it down in the corner. Dusty came running and lapped up most of the liquid. "You were thirsty."

"You seem to know exactly what to do, Trace."

"With a vet for a father, you pick up a few tricks, but it's going to take time to train Dusty to our lifestyle. So far I'd say he's doing great. You need to get to bed. I'll turn out the lights."

"Thank you for an unforgettable evening. I'm thrilled you got a dog."

When Dusty started to follow her out of the kitchen, Trace told him to stay. He stopped in the doorway and made a few strange sounds, but he didn't take another step. Mr. Ogilvie had trained his dog well.

"Good night, Dusty. See you in the morning." She patted his head before disappearing.

"Okay buddy, let's lock up." Dusty stayed by him as he walked around before going to his room. "Here's your bed." He stood by it until the dog curled up in it with one of his toys that looked like a weasel.

Trace got ready for bed and wore the bottom half of his navy sweats. Before he got in, he knelt down to gentle the dog. "We need you a lot more than you need us, Dusty. That woman in the next room needs all the protection we can give her."

After turning out the light, he slid under the covers with a deep sigh. He didn't envy the dog who had undergone a huge change in his life. But as Trace's father had told him, even if a dog had a long memory, he would adjust fast if given love and attention. He and Cassie could supply that in abundance.

He drifted off with visions of Cassie running through his mind. But sometime during the night he was awakened by low moans that made him jump out of bed. Dusty wasn't in his bed. Trace left the bedroom and found the dog outside Cassie's door. He'd put his paws as far under the slit as possible. Trace had to smother his laughter.

I know how you feel, he spoke to himself. *I want to crawl into her bed, too, but we can't. You have to be invited.*

"Come to bed, Dusty." The dog made another moaning sound, but he obeyed Trace. "Stay," he said after he got back in his little bed.

Ten minutes later the moaning started up again. Through the slits of his eyes he noticed the dog was missing again. Once more he got up and walked down the hall. But this time Cassie opened her door dressed in a robe that revealed her swollen figure. Her hair was beautiful, all disheveled and golden.

"Are you lonesome tonight, Dusty?" She darted Trace a glance. "I know he needs to learn his place, but do you think it would be all right if I sit by his bed for a few minutes so he'll settle down? Otherwise you're not going to get any sleep either."

How could he possibly tell her no when she looked at him with eyes as pleading as the dog's?

"Come to bed, Dusty," he told him. Cassie followed them to his bedroom and sat down on the floor next to the doggie bed. Dusty lay down on his back with his paws up, another peculiarity they found endearing. Trace sat next to her. The dog had gotten his way. In the end he was thankful for Dusty because an hour later, Cassie had fallen into a sound sleep against Trace's shoulder.

He put his arm around her and lowered her head to

the floor, leaving his arm there for a cushion. She turned into him, bringing her body breathlessly close to his.

The world in his arms.

That's what it felt like. In a minute he'd waken her so she could go back to bed. But for this moment he wanted to savor her sweetness a little longer.

When the sleeping dog whimpered, Cassie stirred and her eyes opened. "Trace?" she whispered, sounding disoriented.

"You fell asleep."

Her free hand had been resting against his chest. Now that she was waking up, she started to touch him experimentally. "For how long?"

"About an hour."

"I'm sorry."

"I'm not. You were out like a light and needed the sleep."

"You're so good to me."

Their mouths were achingly close. He brushed his lips against hers out of need. "It's because you're so easy to please I want to do everything for you."

"Trace..." This time she took the initiative and pressed her lips against his. That was all it took to deprive him of his last shred of self-control. Maybe he was dreaming, but her mouth seemed to welcome his, urging him to kiss her and hold nothing back.

He pulled her against him, loving the shape of her, the fragrance of her hair, the softness of her skin. She'd aroused his passion on so many levels, he didn't know how he was going to stop, but he had to. He could feel her baby. Much as he wanted to make love to her, he couldn't. This wasn't the time, and the floor wasn't the place. Cassie needed to be able to trust him.

Let go of her now, Rafferty.

As carefully as he could, he eased her away from him and got to his feet. "Even with the carpeting, the floor is hard. Come on. Now that we've got Dusty to bed, it's your turn." He helped her to her feet. She weaved in place. Trace clasped her upper arms until she felt steady.

Her eyes looked glazed as she stared at him in the semidarkness. "I won't pretend I thought you were Logan when I first woke up."

Her honesty slayed him. "Believe it or not, Nicci wasn't in there either."

"Attraction is a dangerous thing."

"Only if it's wrong, but there's nothing wrong with what we just shared."

"Thank you for having more discipline than I do."

He smiled, loving her frank speaking. "If I had control, I wouldn't have let you fall asleep on my shoulder. That makes us even. Let's blame it on nerves over becoming new parents tonight."

To his relief Cassie smiled back. "I like that excuse better than anything you could have come up with besides the truth. I'm going back to bed now. If Dusty whines at my door, I won't open it. He has to learn discipline. Unfortunately his new parents have to teach him 'do as we say, not as we do.'"

But for the dog, Trace would have burst into laughter. Long after she went to her bedroom, Trace lay in his bed knowing he might not get any sleep for what was left of the rest of the night. Cassie had fanned the flame tonight. It was all part of the same fire he'd felt ignite when he'd first found her in the garden.

He knew in his gut she'd felt it, too.

Chapter Nine

Dr. Raynard helped Cassie sit up on the examining table. "After you're ready, come into my office. I want to talk to you."

She hoped nothing was wrong. A little alarmed, Cassie got off the table and straightened her skirt. After reaching for her purse she went into his office and sat down opposite his desk.

"Is there anything wrong?" she asked immediately.

"Your baby is doing fine and we want to keep things that way. But you've developed a condition called pre-eclampsia. For one thing, your blood pressure is higher than I'd like to see it.

"Are you under any undue pressure lately that could have contributed to it since your last exam?"

"Yes." Ned had come home, but she didn't want to talk to the doctor about her brother. Everyone in her family was trying to do something about it. Trace had gotten them a dog to ease her anxiety. She loved that man to distraction.

"I'm sorry to hear it. You must have noticed you have more swelling."

"Yes. What can I do?"

"Don't salt any food and lie down between your normal household activities."

"But I've got a job at a beauty salon."

"I'm afraid you'll have to quit. We want to keep your blood pressure from elevating."

Cassie couldn't believe it. "Can I take walks with my horse and dog?"

"Once a day. A short walk. Ten minutes, no longer."

"I've been doing volunteer work at the wildlife sanctuary on Saturdays."

"No more of that, no grocery shopping, no rides in the car. Let someone else do any errands."

I can't do that to Trace.

"What aren't you telling me, doctor? This is really serious, isn't it."

"It can be if you ignore it. But if you'll mind me, you'll be fine. As a precaution I want to see you weekly for a urine sample and blood pressure check until the baby is born. You're at twenty-four weeks now. I'm hoping you can go as close to term as possible."

Panic had taken over. "What if I can't?"

"If it looks necessary, we might have to do a Cesarean. There's only one cure for this condition. That's to give birth. Until then we take every precaution to ensure a healthy mom and baby. Go home and relax as much as you can. You're in excellent condition in every other way. Continue to take care of yourself and I know things will be fine."

She wished she had his faith.

"Do you have any more questions I can answer?"

"What are the chances of the baby surviving if you have to take her early?"

"Don't worry about that right now, Cassie. Just concentrate on rest. Watch TV, read some good books, listen to music. Those are distractions that will alleviate some of your stress."

Nothing was going to relieve her fear while Ned was out there. She got to her feet. "Thanks, Dr. Raynard. I'll follow your advice. This baby means everything to me."

"Of course it does. See you next Friday."

Cassie left the clinic in such a different frame of mind, she didn't know which foot to put in front of the other. For the moment she had to get back to work until Mildred relieved her. Then Cassie would drop her bomb. She hated having to let the owner down. It meant Mildred would have to advertise for someone else, but Cassie's precious baby had to come first.

At three-thirty she left the beauty salon for the last time. Mildred had been so kind and understanding. Cassie drove her truck down the alley and headed for Zane and Avery's ranch. She needed to find out if their offer still stood to let her stay with them until the baby was born. To put any more burden on Trace was out of the question.

After what happened the night they'd brought Dusty home, she needed to put space between them anyway. When Trace had started kissing her, she'd spun out of control. It still embarrassed her that he'd been the one to bring a halt to the rapture she'd experienced for those unforgettable moments in his arms.

For the past week they'd been friendly and had spent

any free time together playing with Dusty. The dog was a great buffer to prevent her from getting too close to Trace, who kept his distance without being obvious. Despite the desire they both felt, he respected her pregnant condition. His gallantry was a revelation.

She'd been so happy since he'd come home from Italy. Who could have foreseen a health problem this serious that forced her to seek Avery's help after all? If not hers, then maybe Millie Henson would be willing to let her live with them and pay rent until after the baby was born.

Cassie should have known this past heavenly month with Trace couldn't continue. Tears rolled down her cheeks while she took the turnoff for Zane's ranch. If Avery wasn't home yet, she'd wait for her out in front. Maybe she ought to seek out Millie right now, but Cassie needed someone to talk to first. Avery was like a sister.

When she turned in to the ranch her heart leaped to see the Explorer just leaving. Trace put on his brakes and drew alongside her. He was the last person she'd expected to see. She didn't have time to wipe her wet face before he scrutinized her.

His brows furrowed. "What's wrong? Did Owen or Ned do something while you were at the salon?"

She wiped her cheeks. "No. I came to see Avery."

"Zane said she wouldn't be home until later." Cassie groaned. "How did your doctor's appointment go?"

"Fine. What are you doing here? Where's Dusty?"

"In the kennel for a little while. If anyone comes around, he'll bark and hopefully warn an intruder off. I've just picked up some surveillance cameras Zane bought for me to install on the property. When we're both away from the house, anyone who trespasses will be caught on video. I'll follow you home and mount them."

Trace was doing everything in his power to relieve her fear. The only thing she could do to repay him for his goodness was to move out so he could get on with his life. She couldn't bear for him to have to wait on her because she knew he would treat her like a princess. Since she wanted to talk to Avery before she did anything, Cassie turned the truck around and drove back to the ranch.

Once parked, she hurried inside the house and ran to her room. After sitting on the side of her bed, she phoned Avery but had to leave a message on her voice mail. Cassie asked her to call her when she could, then hung up.

She made one more call to the sanctuary. When she told the owner she wouldn't be able to volunteer until after the baby was born, Adrian thanked Cassie profusely for all her help and wished her the very best. She made Cassie promise to visit with the baby when she was able to go out.

Lindsey wasn't home when Cassie phoned her. She left a message telling her the doctor told her not to volunteer anymore until after the baby was born. With those phone calls made, she went to the kitchen for a cold lemonade and a bologna sandwich. She made an extra one for Trace.

After reaching in the bag for a doggie treat, she grabbed the leash and went out the back door to find

Dusty. He barked excitedly when he saw her approach the kennel. She gave him a peanut butter doggie bone, then let him out and walked him around the front of the house.

Trace was up on the ladder mounting one of the cameras. Between his powerful legs sheathed in jeans and the muscles that played across his back beneath his white T-shirt while he worked, she was mesmerized.

The dog led her around the ladder. "Dusty wants to be with you."

He looked down at her, impaling her with those blue eyes. "I know, but this isn't the right time. We'll play in a little while, Dusty."

The dog barked.

"He understood you! He's so affectionate."

"We have Mr. Ogilvie to thank for that."

And Trace's kindness. "When you're hungry, I've made you a sandwich. I hope you like bologna and cheese."

"I like everything you fix."

Cassie knew he was waiting for an explanation of her earlier tears, but she would wait until Avery called her back. When she told Trace everything, she wanted her plans to be a fait accompli.

"Come with me, Dusty."

She climbed the front steps and sat down on the swing. The dog jumped up next to her and put his head in her lap. There wasn't much room for him and the baby, too. She played with him. Anyone looking in on the situation would think they were a real family enjoying a lazy summer evening together.

A pain pierced Cassie's heart. There was so much

wrong with this picture. Trace only had partial vision in one eye and was attempting to get over a broken heart. Cassie had to quit her job so she could hope to keep the baby Logan would never see. Her brother was out there somewhere stalking her. Dusty was grieving for his original owner.

Hoping Avery would return her call soon, she put her head back and closed her eyes. Long before she heard the sound of a truck, Dusty started barking and jumped to the porch floor. That pulled the leash out of her hand, bringing her fully awake.

"Dusty! Stay!" she called to him, but he'd already run out to the parking area and barked at Zane and Avery who got out of their truck. Cassie walked down the steps and caught hold of the leash. "It's okay, Dusty. These are friends."

Zane grinned. "That's a great little watchdog you've got there."

"Come and meet him."

After Dusty sniffed them, he stayed by Cassie.

"Look at that," Avery murmured. "He's adorable. I love his coloring."

"He has a blue eye and a brown eye."

"I noticed. You're an original aren't you?" Avery patted his head and he licked her hand.

"While you three have fun, I'll go see what Trace is up to."

Once Zane disappeared around the side of the house, Avery glanced at Cassie. "You sounded serious on the phone earlier. Tell me what's wrong."

The tears started again. "I'm so glad you're here."

Avery hugged her before they went up the steps to the swing and sat down. Dusty sat at Cassie's feet. "I went to my doctor's appointment today. The news wasn't good."

For the next few minutes she poured out her heart to Avery, who was the best listener in the world. "It was one thing to stay here as housekeeper for Trace until the baby came, but I can't do that now. Would you still be willing to let me stay with you? I'll pay rent."

"Do you even have to ask? As for rent, you're crazy. I told you that when I learned you were pregnant, you would always have a home with me and Zane until you were on your feet again. Have you told Trace yet?"

She averted her eyes. "No. He saw me crying earlier and knows something's wrong, but I needed to talk to you first."

"Are you prepared for him to protest your going anywhere else?"

"That'll be the Good Samaritan in him talking. But you don't know Trace the way I do. He'll become a full-time caretaker, doctor, nurse, cook, breadwinner. He didn't sign on for that kind of responsibility when he decided to go back to ranching again. I was hired to keep the house up and fix his meals, not the other way around."

"What if he wants to be all those things?"

"You're not serious!" she exclaimed.

"Maybe it's because you're too close to it, but Zane and I have noticed a change in Trace over the last few weeks, a contentment. I think helping you has pulled him out of that deep depression since his injury. Zane told me he isn't the same morose man he was a month ago when he dropped in with Jarod, determined to sell the ranch.

"Frankly, you're not the same depressed woman, either. You'll have to look at the video Mac took of everyone at the shower. Anyone watching the two of you wouldn't have a clue there was any sadness in either of you. Something tells me that if you tell him you're leaving, his PTSD could act up."

"You know about that?"

"A lot."

"What does that mean, Avery?"

"Only my brothers and Zane know what I'm about to confide. Since you're like my sister, I'm going to tell you. I was assaulted by a man who's in prison now. It happened when I went to college in Bozeman."

"Avery—" Cassie hugged her for a long time. So many things suddenly made sense that had never made sense before she married Zane.

"I've had to live with my PTSD and Zane's. We've seen it in Trace. It wasn't just the injury to his eye. He suffered severe trauma when his parents divorced. Not all children of divorce react that way. My psychiatrist told me you don't just get PTSD in war. I can tell that living with you is helping him to heal."

Was it true?

"Cassie, when I've talked to my therapist about you, she told me you've been dealing with PTSD, too. The trauma of your family life was bad enough. But when Uncle Grant ordered you out of the house, you went through a life-changing crisis. Logan's death only added to it. You need to heal. I've seen how you respond to Trace. It's my belief you two need each other. Don't worry about the future. Just take it a day at a time."

Avery didn't know what she was asking. But since she'd been through the most horrific experience a woman could face, Cassie knew there was a lot of wisdom in her cousin.

"I'll think about what you've said." She hugged her hard.

"Good. But like I said, you can come home to us if that's what you decide."

"Thank you. Have you had dinner yet?"

"No."

"Then come in the house. I'll make some more sandwiches and whip up a salad."

"That sounds good."

"Come on, Dusty. Let's go inside. I'm sure you need water." He barked, causing Cassie to laugh. "Trace swears he understands everything."

Avery's eyebrows lifted. "Did he suggest getting the dog?"

"Yes. He had a collie years ago."

"I remember. Sounds like he's over the pain of losing his dog. Connor told me he was so broken up, it changed him into a much more serious guy. He swore he'd never own another one again."

Cassie's breath caught. "When did it happen?"

"Soon after his mother moved to Billings and he had to go with her."

Dusty echoed Cassie's moan as they went in the house.

AROUND NINE, TRACE walked in the back door. Dusty rushed out of the kitchen to greet him. "The last camera has been mounted on the exterior of the barn."

"Great!" Cassie was sweeping the kitchen floor. Zane and Avery had just left after he'd helped mount a camera over the back door. "Between those and Dusty, you've got us covered."

"That's the plan." He walked over to the sink and washed his hands. While he dried them, he looked at her. "Want to take in a late movie in White Lodge? A James Bond film I understand. I never did see all of them."

She put the broom in the closet. "I'd like to, but I can't."

"Why?"

Cassie had been mulling over Avery's words in her mind all evening. "Why don't we go in the living room?"

In an instant, stress lines marred his striking features. He went ahead of her, but he didn't sit when she sank down on the couch. Dusty wandered around the room with a toy. "I've been waiting until we were alone to find out why you were in tears earlier."

"No one deserves an explanation more than you do. Today at my appointment, the doctor told me I've developed a condition called preeclampsia."

"I've heard of it. One of the pilots in my squadron had a wife who suffered from it."

"How did it turn out for her?"

"Fine. But she had to go to bed for eight months of her pregnancy."

Eight?

"So I guess you have a good idea of what my doctor told me I have to do."

"Yup. I'm going to turn into Mr. Mom."

His comment was so unexpected, she laughed. "I'm being serious now, Trace."

"So am I. Did he tell you to quit your job?"

"Yes. I already did it today."

"Good."

"Trace—if I continue to stay here, my activities are limited." She listed everything so he'd understand exactly. "I'm supposed to be working for you, remember?"

He smiled. "Did your doctor know he was talking to the most independent mother-to-be in Montana? Does he know how drastic this is going to be for you to let someone else help take care of you?"

Trace knew her better than she knew herself. "I don't imagine any woman likes hearing it."

"Especially you, but I'll help you pass the time. It won't be so bad." If only he knew how heavenly that sounded.

"You don't have to do this, Trace. I talked to Avery and can move there tomorrow."

He rubbed the back of his neck. "Knowing how your mind works, whom would you rather inconvenience? The Lawsons or yours truly?"

"That's not a fair question because there's no good answer."

"Why don't you think about where you'll be happiest and give me your decision tomorrow? But I'd rather you stayed here so you can walk me through the process of putting up raspberry jam. They're starting to ripen. I'll set up a sun lounger in the kitchen. You can lie there with your feet up and give me instructions."

"You'd actually do that?"

"Whatever it takes to entertain you until your daughter arrives. Have you thought of a name yet?"

"I *have*." While he was mounting the camera in front, it came to her.

"And?"

"I'm going to think about it for a while before I say it out loud."

"So you're superstitious?" he asked playfully.

"No. I've just got to be sure. Trace—if I stay here, you have to promise you'll let me pay you the money I was going to use for the first and last month's rent on that apartment. I have it and more saved in the bank."

"Agreed." He answered too fast. "Do we have a deal?"

Her heart pounded so hard she felt sick. "Only if *you're* sure."

He flicked her another glance. "Do you honestly think I would have bothered to get a dog if I hadn't planned on you being here throughout your pregnancy? Dusty will go into mourning if he can't find you tomorrow."

Trace knew how to apply emotional bribery to her exact vulnerable area.

"Any other conditions before I send you to bed where you should have been an hour ago? Considering everything you've done since you left the doctor's office, you've already disobeyed his instructions."

"I'm aware of that."

"If you want to know the truth, I've been hoping you won't leave. I like having you around. That first day I

got home from Italy, I dreaded driving out here knowing I'd be bombarded with too many memories I didn't
want to think about. But the minute I saw you in the
fruit garden and realized the pain you were living with,
they seemed to vanish.

"Now that we've got Dusty and your pregnancy is
coming along, it feels good to be alive despite my bad
eye, your brother and maybe even momnesia."

Avery had been right about everything.

"I'd like to stay, but only on the condition that if it
gets too hard, Avery will insist on taking over."

CONNOR AND TRACE rode Buttercup and Masala to the
pasture to exercise the horses. Before Cassie had been
put to bed, he'd planned to have a herd of cattle un-
loaded. But the situation had forced him to put any of
those ranching ideas on hold.

"I went to the checkup with her this morning. While
she was in the restroom, I spoke to Dr. Raynard. After
eight weeks of virtual bed rest, her blood pressure is
even higher and there's too much protein in her urine.
He's given her a medication to help. If it can get her
to last another week, then he'll perform a Cesarean."

"That's too early," Connor muttered.

"He says that at thirty-three weeks the baby will be
in good shape. I need to be on hand because once she's
born, the baby could be in the hospital a month or longer and Cassie will want to be right there with her. He
wants me to bring her in day after tomorrow to see if
the medicine is helping. That's why I haven't done anything about the cattle yet."

"I hear you."

"What's the word on Ned?"

"We've noticed him riding around the ranch with my uncle. Jarod caught sight of him headed into the mountains alone the other day and followed him until he came back. I saw him driving with Owen in Owen's truck yesterday."

"Did they leave the ranch?"

Connor nodded. "I followed them into White Lodge. They hit the supermarket. I'll give you one guess what they bought. Then they drove to the Pearson ranch. I stayed hidden and followed them after they left to bring Ned back. Jarod and I are doing our damndest to keep an eye on him. It's clear my uncle hasn't put him to work yet, which means he's still afraid of his son and Ned is the same old Ned."

"Cassie never believed he would change. Now he's free to come and go. I check the video on the cameras every day. So far, neither Ned or Owen have trespassed, unless they're aware of the cameras and move out of the line of vision."

"We simply don't know what Ned's up to. I've talked to Zane. He's no closer to finding the person who shot Logan, but we're all keeping a close eye on Ned."

"You can't do more than that, Connor. If he gets into one of his manic moods, he'll make a mistake and we'll be ready for him."

"Liz and her mom are planning on taking turns with the girls to help when the time comes."

"You've all done so much already bringing food and keeping her company. Cassie is so grateful."

"My cousin didn't deserve all that's happened to her. Thank God she has you, Trace. Let's get back to her."

"Do you ever talk to Cassie's mother?"

"No. She stays away. The only time I see her is when she leaves the ranch. Her mother still lives in Bozeman and she goes there a lot."

Trace shook his head.

"Don't try to figure it out, Trace. It's Cassie she should be visiting and giving comfort to. I think living with my uncle and Ned did something to her mind a long, long time ago. Jarod's convinced of it."

On that tragic note they galloped back to give the horses a workout. When they reached the paddock, Connor took off in his truck. Trace watered their mounts and left them to graze while he hurried toward the house. He could hear Dusty's bark before he entered through the back door.

"Hey, buddy. Let's go see how Cassie's doing."

He found her on the couch in the living room with her jean-clad legs propped. Her blond hair fanned around her head on the pillow. She was one woman whose body hadn't looked that pregnant at six months. But over the past two the baby had really grown.

"Sorry we were gone so long. Are you ready for dinner?"

"Whenever you are. It's disgusting how I can lie around all day and still be hungry for every meal. Did I tell you my little girl has found a new place to jab me? She did it during the night and now she's at it again. Here. Feel *this*."

His pulse raced. Trace had been hoping she'd let him

feel the baby again. He hadn't dared touch her since the night he'd wanted to go on kissing her senseless. That seemed like a century ago. After she'd left his arms to go to bed, he'd forced himself to put his desire for her in cold storage.

But now that she'd just given him permission, he hunkered down next to her. She took his hand and put it on the side of her swollen belly. He felt movement at once, hard and strong. "Good grief. That has to hurt!"

"It kind of does now that she's been doing it in the same place for so long. I need to shift positions." He had to give her credit for trying. "Do you have any idea how difficult it is to move when you feel like a beached porpoise?"

"Don't you mean whale?"

Her eyes rounded. "Do I look that huge?"

He chuckled over her hurt expression. "No, Cassie. No. You look good enough to eat," he whispered. Without waiting for permission, he covered her mouth with his own, breaking the rule he'd set for himself two months ago. He couldn't help it.

For a pregnant woman who was more or less stuck in that position, her hungry response sent *his* blood pressure spiking through the roof. Neither of them could get enough of the other. Cassie was with him all the way. His patience was paying off.

Don't blow it now, Rafferty.

He finally lifted his mouth from hers, struggling for breath. She made a little groan of protest that thrilled him. But he was far too conscious of her medical condition to take advantage of the moment. Instead he gripped one of her hands.

"You're so lovely, I couldn't resist. Don't say another word about how you look. There's a glow about you I find irresistible. You're going to make the most stunning mother."

"I hope you know your compliments are spoiling me."

"Good. Connor said you were the most popular girl at high school and I believe it."

"He made that up."

"Nope. I heard it from Jarod, too."

"Thanks for trying to cheer me up." Fear had entered her eyes. "You really think the baby will be all right being born premature?"

"Believe your doctor. Even if it came today, he said both of you would be fine." Overwhelmed by love for her, Trace drew her into his arms and pressed his cheek against her hot one. "You're going to have a beautiful baby."

"I just want her to be healthy," she said as Dusty started barking.

"Someone's at the door."

Trace had been so involved with Cassie, he hadn't heard a knock or the doorbell. "Just a minute and let me see who it is." He sprang to his feet and strode to the front door. When he opened it, he discovered his father and Ellen standing there with food they'd brought. He invited them inside. No sight could have been more welcome.

While they hugged, Dusty brushed up against Sam

who leaned over to pet him. "You remember me, don't you, boy. Do you like your new home?" The dog barked.

"He was talking to you, Sam." This from Cassie.

"Cassie has me convinced he really does talk," Trace exclaimed. "How did you two know Cassie and I were hungry for dinner? Something smells delicious."

Ellen smiled. "I'll fix a plate for everyone and we'll eat in here."

A few minutes later they settled down to enjoy the fajitas she'd made. Trace told them what the doctor had said. His father leaned forward in his chair.

"Cassie? I understand your fears, but thousands of women face this and come out of it fine. Your doctor knows what he's doing. Remember—you've been through the worst part having to stay on bed rest."

"I disagree. Your son is the one whose life has been living torture. He's worn every hat there is taking care of me and has listened to me cry and worry until I'm sure he's ready to scream. Both of you should get a medal."

Sam looked surprised. "What do I have to do with it?"

"You raised him to be as exceptional as you are."

"She's right," Ellen chimed in.

Trace had rarely seen his father blush. He was glad his dad had come over tonight. Cassie had never needed reassurance more. When they were ready to leave she said, "Ellen? Take one of those jars of raspberry jam home with you. Trace made it."

"He did?"

"She told me what to do," Trace explained. "It all

sold at the White Lodge fair, but I held a few jars back for us."

"We're both impressed." Sam gave Cassie a kiss on the cheek. After hugging Trace, they left. He could tell their visit had relaxed her.

"What can I do for you?" he asked after shutting the door.

"You and Dusty can watch football to your heart's content while I go to bed." She got up from the couch with some difficulty. "Your dad and Ellen are the greatest. See you in the morning."

He didn't try to detain her. Trace could tell she was tired. Hopefully she'd fall right to sleep and not brood over her condition.

Chapter Ten

The next afternoon Cassie lay on the couch watching TV. She'd worn a robe over her nightgown because she was more comfortable like that at this stage in her pregnancy. Dusty suddenly sprang from the floor where he'd been lying in front of her and flew out of the living room, barking so loudly it startled her. She sat up as carefully as she could.

When he came back, he headed straight for the front door and wouldn't stop barking.

"What is it, Dusty?" For the dog to go investigate meant someone had been walking around the outside of the house. Trace had driven over to Connor's and said he'd be right back. Dusty would never react like that if it were Trace returning in the truck. She would have heard the engine.

The dog darted from the door to the front window. His front paws rested on the window sill. His bark had turned into a primitive growl, his tail high in the air. It caused the hairs to lift on the back of her neck. She shut off the TV with the remote.

Someone had been prowling around that Dusty didn't

recognize. Cassie hadn't heard the bell or a knock. Whoever it was had started rapping on the big window, obviously enjoying baiting the dog. She got to her swollen feet.

When she padded over to the window to look out, she got the fright of her life. A man stood there on the front porch in front of the window, pressing his face against the glass. Though his features were distorted, she'd know him anywhere.

Ned.

Her body started trembling with fear and wouldn't stop. Any meds he'd been on either weren't working, or he hadn't taken them. His manic side was in full evidence. She moved away from the window and flattened her back against the wall where he could no longer see her. Dusty stayed on point, growling with menace.

Fear caused her body to break out in a cold sweat.

Come home, Trace. Please, God.

"I already saw you through the window, Cassie. Don't you know you can't hide from me?" he taunted. "Especially when you're fat as a French hen with that bastard's baby."

Knowing he was out there made her physically ill. "What are you doing here?" she called to him, praying not to show how terrified she was. Her cell phone was on the end table, a couple of yards away. If she lunged for it, he would see her.

"That's a fine way to speak to your brother. Not even a hello after all this time?"

"Go away, Ned. You're not welcome here."

"It's no sin to come and see my sister, is it?" Suddenly he was trying to open the front door. He kept it up, trying to force his way in with the strength of his body. Snarling, Dusty dashed to the door and barked his head off. But neither of them would be a match for her brother, who was like an animal gone berserk. There was no reasoning with him.

She hurried over to the table and grabbed the phone to call Trace. Her fingers shook, making it difficult to press the digit. *Answer it!* But it went to his voice mail.

"Help, Trace—Ned's here! He's trying to break in!"

Ned was at the window again and could see her. "I know what you're doing, little sister. But there's no Logan to help you now. I should have gotten rid of him before you disgraced our family with his kid."

So he *had* killed Logan!

"Now it's time to get rid of you."

Her brother was in a full rage. Cassie had the sure knowledge that he was going to kill her, too. Forgetting she was pregnant, she ran over to the fireplace. She had to stretch to take the rifle from the rack. Trace didn't keep it loaded. The ammunition was in the drawer of the credenza, but Ned didn't know that. It could buy her some time until Trace got here.

The dog kept up his blood-curdling growl until she heard glass shatter, then a yelp. Ned had used the end of a shotgun to break the pane.

"Dusty!"

Her brother pushed out the rest of the glass before climbing inside the living room. He stepped over the dog who lay moaning in pain and lifted the shotgun to his shoulder. Out of self-preservation she dropped to the floor with Trace's rifle and turned on her side away from him.

Not my baby. Not my baby.

She shuddered in horror as Ned walked around so he was facing her with those soulless eyes glittering down at her. "You have no idea how many years I've wanted to do this." He pointed the shotgun straight at her. "The perfect sister who always did everything right. The popular one. But you made a big mistake when you married Logan."

Somehow she found the strength to send the rifle hurtling against his knee caps.

He let out a groan. "Damn if you aren't a regular little hellcat. Let's see if you like the way *this* feels." Turning the butt end of the shotgun around, he moved toward her with only one intention. To smash her and her unborn baby to pulp. She got up from the floor and ran screaming Trace's name at the top of her lungs.

"I'm here!" came the beloved voice.

Trace had come in through the front door. He swept her into his arms and rocked her close to him. "You're safe now, sweetheart."

She could hear her cousins' voices mingled with Ned's threats in the background, but nothing mattered because Trace had come for her. "I'm getting you to the hospital right now." He carried her out of the house to his Explorer parked in front.

"Thank God you came when you did," she said after he'd settled her in the front seat. "I think I've hurt the baby."

"You're going to be fine. Dr. Raynard is meeting us there."

Tears streamed down her cheeks. "Ned admitted he killed Logan."

"He's not ever going to hurt anyone again. The camera videotape will have caught him climbing the porch steps with the shotgun. It will provide the positive proof Zane has been looking for. He and your cousins are taking care of Ned right now."

She shook her head. "To think my only brother is so mentally ill. I'm having a hard time conceiving it. I wonder what my parents are going to think now," she half moaned.

"Cassie—your mother called Connor and told him Ned sneaked out of the house. He's been refusing to take his medication. Your dad went to look for him. She was worried sick for you and begged everyone to find Ned and stop him before he reached you."

"Mother did that?"

"Yes. We have her to thank that we got to my ranch in time to save you."

"I—I can't believe it."

"Believe it, Cassie. She loves you and is devastated by what has been going on all these years. Now that Ned is going to be taken care of, she can concentrate on loving and helping you."

"I want that more than anything." She wiped her eyes. "What about Dusty? I'm afraid the glass really hurt him."

"He'll be all right after Dad takes a look at him. Hang on, Cassie. We're almost there."

"Because it's you, I'll hang on for as long as it takes."

She felt him grasp her hand and hold it the rest of the way.

TWENTY-FOUR HOURS LATER the nurse wheeled Cassie down the hall to the NICU. Trace's tall, hard-muscled physique was waiting inside the unit. He'd been gowned, gloved and masked. So much love poured out of her, there were no words to describe how she felt about him at this point.

Dr. Raynard had done a Cesarean after she'd reached the hospital. Cassie's baby weighed in at four pounds, elating her and the doctor. The pediatrician proclaimed her in excellent health considering her early arrival.

Cassie had started to pump her breast milk. They fed it to the baby through a tube in her mouth. The incubator kept her warm. Both Trace and Cassie could reach in the holes to hold the baby's little fingers and talk to her.

Beneath his black hair and brows, Trace's eyes were a brilliant blue above the face mask he wore. "She's so tiny and perfect. With her fine blond hair, she looks a lot like you, Cassie."

"I just can't believe she's here," she said through the mask. "It's over. Thanks to you, I have her and my life." Her voice shook. "I owe you everything, Trace."

"Everyone pitched in. It was a team effort. Even Dusty tried to help."

"How is he?"

"Dad had to put a couple of stitches in his left ear. He's doing well, but is going to stay with my father and Ellen for a while."

"The poor little darling. You can't believe how fierce he was when he saw Ned out on the porch. He's really a great watchdog." After a pause she said, "So are you." Emotion had caught up to her. "Where did you come from, Trace Rafferty? How was I ever so blessed? You've had to wait on me day and night for months and have put up with me when I was grumpy and out of sorts. You have the temperament of a saint."

"Really? Then it's good you didn't hear me when I reamed out Lamont Walker."

"He was awful."

"I didn't like him on sight. But let's not talk about unpleasant things anymore. How soon does the doctor think you can take her home?"

"Maybe two weeks. She has to be able to suck on a bottle. They're watching her sleep habits and checking for infections."

"How soon can *you* come home?"

Cassie didn't have a home yet. She was living in Trace's home out of the goodness of his generous heart. "I think tomorrow after the doctor does his rounds, if he thinks I'm recovered enough. But I'll only be there to sleep before I go back to the hospital and be with the baby."

"We'll do it together."

Though music to her ears, he had other obligations. Now he could start putting his plans for the ranch into action. But she refrained from reminding him. Her momnesia had taken over and she couldn't think about anything but this miracle that had happened.

Ten days later Trace brought her and the baby home.

When they entered the nursery, she saw a new rocking chair in the corner the same color as the crib. "Oh, Trace—I love it!"

"This is my welcome home present to you. Now you'll be comfortable feeding her."

He'd turned the bedroom into a nursery for her precious daughter who was putting on a little weight every day. As Trace helped her put the sleeping baby in the crib and she realized there was nothing more to fear from Ned, Cassie felt euphoric. Forget that the Cesarean had caused her any discomfort and made her a little slower on her feet, she couldn't complain about anything.

Cassie looked at him. "You've been here from the beginning. I owe you my life, Trace."

"I was just thinking the same thing about you. When I came home from Italy, my depression was so bad at the time, I knew Nicci and I wouldn't be able to work things out. I figured I'd never have the experience of being a husband and parent. But you let me be a part of yours. Whether right or wrong, that sonogram picture did something to me."

"It felt natural to show it to you," she admitted.

"The times you let me feel the baby moving brought me alive again. At the hospital you asked the doctor if I could come in to watch the procedure."

"You'd been with me every step of the way. I couldn't imagine you not being a part of her birth."

"It felt like you were pregnant with my child. When I saw the baby lifted out of you and heard your cry of joy, it touched something in my soul."

"Mine, too." Her fingers gripped the crib railing. "I want to show you something. If you'd go to my bedroom and look in the closet, the little wooden toy chest is there. Would you bring it in here?"

Trace had wondered where it had been all this time. He couldn't imagine why she'd put it in there. Though her request seemed odd, he didn't question it. "I'll be right back."

He hurried down the hall to her bedroom and opened the closet door. Mystified, he found it at the back hiding behind some clothes. When he pulled it out, he saw that she'd transformed it with her unique artwork. She must have painted it whenever he left the house to do errands.

But when he brought it out of the closet, he stopped because he saw the name she'd painted on the center of the lid.

Tracey.

He needed a minute to get himself under control before he carried it to the nursery. She looked up at him with a hint of anxiety. "Do you like her name?"

Trace was overcome. "I don't know what to say." His voice sounded husky to his own ears.

"I painted it right after you gave it to me. In my heart she's been Tracey for a long time."

Her eyes glistened. "It's to honor the most wonderful man I know. I've known quite a few, but your name is at the top of that remarkable list. When my daughter is old enough, I'm going to tell her how I came to give it to her."

He put the toy box down on the floor and pulled something from his pocket. "Come here." He drew her over to the rocking chair, but he sat down first before pulling her onto his lap. "Cassie?" His breath was warm against her neck.

By now she was trembling like crazy. "Yes?"

"I have something for you. Hold up your left hand."

Could this really be happening?

"I've waited a long time to do this." He reached around and pushed a diamond set in gold on her ring finger. "You're going to marry me, right? You *have* to. I'm madly in love with you and I want to adopt Tracey. My two Montana cowgirls. If you don't tell me what I want to hear, I won't be able to handle it."

She didn't answer him right away. He shouldn't have done it yet, but he hadn't been able to hold back.

"Cassie?" he prodded her. "Say something—"

Hearing his uncertainty, she got up from his lap and turned around, placing her hands on the arms of the chair. Her eyes had ignited with little green fires. "After we're married, I'll have the birth certificate amended to read Tracey Dorney *Rafferty*. How does that sound?"

"Sweetheart—"

Before she knew it, he'd picked her up and walked her the few feet to the bed. He followed her down on it, taking care not to hurt her.

"Cassie—if you only knew how long I've wanted to be able to just hold you like this and not worry that you'd tell me it was too soon."

"Too soon?" She laughed for joy. "I've been desperately in love with you from the moment you walked out to the fruit garden. Sam Rafferty's son was home. When you smiled at me, that was it. There will always be that place in my heart for the Logan of my past life. But when you walked into my world that day looking so gorgeous and wonderful, you changed my life."

He kissed her long and hard. "When shall we get married?"

"Whenever the arrangements can be made."

"Thank heaven. I don't want to waste any more time. Dad once told me that God's mills grind slowly, but they grind. We've been through the hard part and can attest to it, beloved. Now it's time to live."

AFTER A PASSION-FILLED wedding night, Cassie woke up before Trace. His legs had trapped hers and his arm held on to her possessively even though he slept.

She looked around Connor's trailer. This had been his home on the road with Liz while they were building their new ranch house. Since he knew Cassie couldn't be far away from Tracey for a while longer, he offered his trailer as a temporary wedding night solution. He and Liz wanted to take care of the baby for them at Trace's ranch.

Cassie loved this tiny house on wheels. Everything you needed was right here. Best of all it was totally private and so cozy.

At her six weeks' checkup, Dr. Raynard had proclaimed her well and healthy. *Hallelujah*, Trace had shouted before giving her a husband's kiss, hot with the passion they no longer had to hold back. Cassie shared his sentiment so completely all night long, she hardly knew herself.

Trace was the most satisfying lover she could ever

have wanted or imagined. Anxious for him to wake up so they could make love again, she started kissing him. He had a compelling mouth that could send her into rapture.

"Um," he moaned before his eyelids opened. "Is my little wanton awake already?"

Cassie actually blushed.

He chuckled and kissed her neck. "Don't ever be embarrassed for making me the happiest man on earth."

"I hope you'll always feel this way." She covered his eyes and nose and mouth with kisses.

"I sense a new happiness in you, sweetheart. Your mother has turned a corner in her own emotional recovery. You can tell she wants to start over to be your mother and a grandmother to Tracey. With Ned back in the facility for good, maybe your dad will change and start to come around, too. There's always hope. Deep down I know it's what you've wanted."

"You know me so well, it's scary."

"I'm still learning exciting new things about you," he whispered into her profusion of gold hair.

Her whole body went hot. "I think I love you too much."

"Don't ever say those words again. Just show me instead." He rolled her on top of him and the divine ritual of loving and being loved started over again. And again. And again.

* * * * *

COMING NEXT MONTH FROM

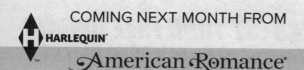

HARLEQUIN®

American Romance®

Available May 5, 2015

#1545 THE COWBOY'S HOMECOMING

Crooked Valley Ranch • by Donna Alward

Rylan Duggan finds himself off the rodeo circuit and back at Crooked Valley Ranch—too close for comfort to Kailey Brandt. She's not about to forgive him for past wrongs, but their chemistry makes him impossible to ignore!

#1546 HER COWBOY GROOM

Blue Falls, Texas • by Trish Milburn

Linnea Holland doesn't trust men anymore. But cowboy Owen Brody shows he has a kind heart beneath his bad-boy exterior and makes her think she *can* trust him—and maybe even fall in love.

#1547 THE RANCHER'S LULLABY

Glades County Cowboys • by Leigh Duncan

Ranch manager and single father Garrett Judd still blames himself for his wife's death. But bluegrass singer Lisa Rose makes embracing life too hard to resist...at least for one stormy night.

#1548 BACK TO TEXAS

Welcome to Ramblewood • by Amanda Renee

Waitress Bridgett Jameson is done being the subject of small-town gossip. Falling for handsome, mysterious ranch hand Adam Steele seems like the perfect escape from Ramblewood...until she learns his secret!

YOU CAN FIND MORE INFORMATION ON UPCOMING HARLEQUIN® TITLES, FREE EXCERPTS AND MORE AT WWW.HARLEQUIN.COM.

HARCNM0415

REQUEST YOUR FREE BOOKS!
2 FREE NOVELS PLUS 2 FREE GIFTS!

HARLEQUIN

American ★ *Romance*

LOVE, HOME & HAPPINESS

Despite still feeling shaky, Linnea descended the steps and started walking. The day was quite warm, but she didn't care. Though she spent most of her time indoors working, there was something therapeutic about getting out in the sunshine under a wide blue sky. It almost made her believe things weren't so bad.

But they were.

She walked the length of the driveway and back. When she approached the house, Roscoe and Cletus, the Brodys' two lovable basset hounds, came ambling around the corner of the porch.

"Hey, guys," she said as she sank onto the front steps and proceeded to scratch them both under their chins. "You're just as handsome as ever."

"Why, thank you."

She jumped at the sound of Owen's voice. The dogs jumped, too, probably because she had. She glanced up to where Owen stood at the corner of the porch. "You made me scare the dogs."

"Sorry. But I was taught to thank someone when they pay me a compliment."

She shook her head. "Nice to see your ego is still intact."

"Ouch."

She laughed a little at his mock affront, something she wouldn't have thought possible that morning. She ought to thank him for that moment of reprieve, but she didn't want to focus on why she'd thought she might never laugh or even smile again.

He tapped the brim of his cowboy hat and headed toward the barn.

As he walked away, she noticed how nice he looked in those worn jeans. No wonder he didn't have trouble finding women.

Oh, hell! She was looking at Owen's butt. Owen, as in Chloe's little brother Owen. The kid who'd once waited on her and Chloe outside Chloe's room and doused them with a Super Soaker, the guy who had earned the nickname Horndog Brody.

She jerked her gaze away, suddenly wondering if she was mentally deficient. First she'd nearly married a guy who was already married. And now, little more than a day after she found out she'd nearly become an unwitting bigamist, she was ogling her best friend's brother's rear end.

Don't miss
HER COWBOY GROOM
by Trish Milburn,
available May 2015 wherever
Harlequin® American Romance®
books and ebooks are sold.

www.Harlequin.com

JUST CAN'T GET ENOUGH?

Join our social communities
and talk to us online.

You will have access to the latest
news on upcoming titles and special
promotions, but most importantly,
you can talk to other fans about your
favorite Harlequin reads.

Harlequin.com/Community

Facebook.com/HarlequinBooks

Twitter.com/HarlequinBooks

Pinterest.com/HarlequinBooks

HARLEQUIN®

A *Romance* FOR EVERY MOOD™

**Stay up-to-date on all your
romance-reading news with the
Harlequin Shopping Guide,
featuring bestselling authors, exciting new
miniseries, books to watch and more!**

The newest issue will be delivered right to you
with our compliments! There are 4 each year.

Signing up is easy.

EMAIL

ShoppingGuide@Harlequin.ca

WRITE TO US

HARLEQUIN BOOKS
Attention: Customer Service Department
P.O. Box 9057, Buffalo, NY 14269-9057

OR PHONE

1-800-873-8635 in the United States
1-888-343-9777 in Canada

Please allow 4-6 weeks for delivery of the first issue by mail.

THE WORLD IS BETTER WITH

Romance

Harlequin has everything from contemporary, passionate and heartwarming to suspenseful and inspirational stories.

Whatever your mood, we have a romance just for you!

Connect with us to find your next great read, special offers and more.